FEMININE PLURAL

FEMININE PLURAL

Stories by Women About Growing Up

EDITED BY STEPHANIE SPINNER

Macmillan Publishing Co., Inc.
New York

ACKNOWLEDGMENTS: "Wunderkind" by Carson McCullers is reprinted by permission of the publisher, Houghton Mifflin Company, from *Collected Short Stories and the Novel The Ballad of the Sad Cafe* by Carson McCullers, Copyright 1955 by Carson McCullers.

"Notes for a Case History" by Doris Lessing is reprinted by permission of Simon and Schuster, Inc., and Curtis Brown Ltd. from *A Man and Two Women* by Doris Lessing, Copyright © 1958, 1962, 1963 by Doris Lessing.

"Green Sealing-Wax" by Colette is reprinted by permission of Farrar, Straus & Giroux, Inc., and Martin Secker & Warburg Ltd. from *The Tender Shoot* by Colette, translated by Antonia White, Copyright © 1958 by Martin Secker & Warburg Ltd.

"Miss Yellow Eyes" by Shirley Ann Grau is reprinted by permission of Alfred A. Knopf, Inc., from *The Black Prince and Other Stories*, by Shirley Ann Grau, Copyright 1954 by Shirley Ann Grau.

"Virgin Violeta" by Katherine Anne Porter is reprinted by permission of Cyrilly Abels, literary agent, from *The Collected Stories of Katherine Anne Porter*, Copyright 1924 by Century Magazine; Copyright renewed 1951 Meredith Publishing Company.

"My First Marriage" by R. Prawer Jhabvala is reprinted by permission of W. W. Norton & Company, Inc., and John Murray (Publishers) Ltd. from *Like Birds, Like Fishes, and Other Stories* by R. Prawer Jhabvala, Copyright © 1963 by R. Prawer Jhabvala.

"Irish Revel" by Edna O'Brien is reprinted by permission of Alfred A. Knopf, Inc., Edna O'Brien and Jonathan Cape Ltd. from *The Love Object* by Edna O'Brien, Copyright © 1962, 1963, 1964, 1965, 1967, 1968 by Edna O'Brien. Originally appeared in *The New Yorker*.

"Your Body Is a Jewel Box" by Kay Boyle is reprinted by permission of New Directions Publishing Corporation from *Thirty Stories* by Kay Boyle, Copyright 1946 by Kay Boyle.

"O Yes" by Tillie Olsen is reprinted by permission of the publisher from *Tell Me a Riddle* by Tillie Olsen, A Seymour Lawrence Book/Delacorte Press, Copyright © 1957 by Tillie Olsen. Originally published in *Prairie Schooner* as "Baptism."

"A Temple of the Holy Ghost" by Flannery O'Connor is reprinted by permission of Harcourt Brace Jovanovich, Inc., from *A Good Man Is Hard to Find* by Flannery O'Connor, Copyright 1954 by Flannery O'Connor.

To Elizabeth Capelle

FOREWORD

Living as we do in a culture that idolizes youth, we are constantly being told that to be young is to be happy. Teenagers "having more fun" smile at us from the pages of every glossy magazine, relaying the message that youth is the best time in life, and that growing up is a completely sunny experience, painless and carefree. Or is it?

The stories in this collection describe the transition from girlhood to womanhood as a time of awakenings and revelations far removed from the popular myths we're exposed to.

In some cases, growing up means the end of romantic illusion. For Mary, in Edna O'Brien's story, the Irish revel produces no handsome stranger, but an assortment of drunken townspeople she must serve in her best lace dress. For Katherine Anne Porter's Violeta, infatuation ends abruptly when her handsome cousin reveals what he thinks of "little girls."

In other stories growing up means learning to compromise with the adult world and its strange, harsh rules of social behavior. Doris Lessing's "Notes for a Case History" is a masterful exposition of one girl's education in bargaining tactics for a "good" marriage; Maureen learns earlier than most that the merchandise she is selling is herself. Tillie Olsen's "O Yes" deals with compromise of another sort, no less chilling because it is unconscious rather than calculated. "Why is it like it is?" asks Carol, bemoaning the loss of her best friend, black. "And why do I have to care?"

And then there is the revelation of sexuality, shattering to the troubled heroine of Kay Boyle's "Your Body Is a Jewel Box," and "the answer to a riddle that was more puzzling than the riddle itself" to the young Southern girl in Flannery O'Connor's comical "A Temple of the Holy Ghost."

Growing up implies progress. Why, then, are so many of these stories about compromise and curtailment, sad beginnings, not happy endings? These writers, these women, speak hard truths; for their characters, some knowingly, some not, are "learning their place" in the adult world. A man's world. Colette's fifteen-year-old retreats back into pigtails and short dresses rather than face it; Shirley Ann Grau's Miss Yellow Eyes can only respond with rage when the rules are set down for her.

In a time when the position of women in society is being reassessed, when old attitudes are being challenged and new ones accepted, these stories have a particular and hopeful relevance. If they are telling us that growth is painful, they also make it clear that dispensing with illusion is the first necessary step on the path to maturity. And that it carries with it its own undeniable rewards.

Stephanie Spinner

CONTENTS

CARSON McCULLERS

Wunderkind

She came into the living room, her music satchel plopping against her winter-stockinged legs and her other arm weighted down with school books, and stood for a moment listening to the sounds from the studio. A soft procession of piano chords and the tuning of a violin. Then Mister Bilderbach called out to her in his chunky, guttural tones:

"That you, Bienchen?"

As she jerked off her mittens she saw that her fingers were twitching to the motions of the fugue she had practiced that morning. "Yes," she answered. "It's me."

"I," the voice corrected. "Just a moment."

She could hear Mister Lafkowitz talking—his words spun

out in a silky, unintelligible hum. A voice almost like a woman's, she thought, compared to Mister Bilderbach's. Restlessness scattered her attention. She fumbled with her geometry book and *Le Voyage de Monsieur Perrichon* before putting them on the table. She sat down on the sofa and began to take her music from the satchel. Again she saw her hands—the quivering tendons that stretched down from her knuckles, the sore finger tip capped with curled, dingy tape. The sight sharpened the fear that had begun to torment her for the past few months.

Noiselessly she mumbled a few phrases of encouragement to herself. A good lesson—a good lesson—like it used to be— Her lips closed as she heard the stolid sound of Mister Bilderbach's footsteps across the floor of the studio and the creaking of the door as it slid open.

For a moment she had the peculiar feeling that during most of the fifteen years of her life she had been looking at the face and shoulders that jutted from behind the door, in a silence disturbed only by the muted, blank plucking of a violin string. Mister Bilderbach. Her teacher, Mister Bilderbach. The quick eyes behind the horn-rimmed glasses; the light, thin hair and the narrow face beneath; the lips full and loose shut and the lower one pink and shining from the bites of his teeth; the forked veins in his temples throbbing plainly enough to be observed across the room.

"Aren't you a little early?" he asked, glancing at the clock on the mantelpiece that had pointed to five minutes of twelve for a month. "Josef's in here. We're running over a little sonatina by someone he knows."

"Good," she said, trying to smile. "I'll listen." She could

see her fingers sinking powerless into a blur of piano keys. She felt tired—felt that if he looked at her much longer her hands might tremble.

He stood uncertain, halfway in the room. Sharply his teeth pushed down on his bright, swollen lip. "Hungry, Bienchen?" he asked. "There's some apple cake Anna made, and milk."

"I'll wait till afterward," she said. "Thanks."

"After you finish with a very fine lesson—eh?" His smile seemed to crumble at the corners.

There was a sound from behind him in the studio and Mister Lafkowitz pushed at the other panel of the door and stood beside him.

"Frances?" he said, smiling. "And how is the work coming now?"

Without meaning to, Mister Lafkowitz always made her feel clumsy and overgrown. He was such a small man himself, with a weary look when he was not holding his violin. His eyebrows curved high above his sallow, Jewish face as though asking a question, but the lids of his eyes drowsed languorous and indifferent. Today he seemed distracted. She watched him come into the room for no apparent purpose, holding his pearl-tipped bow in his still fingers, slowly gliding the white horsehair through a chalky piece of rosin. His eyes were sharp bright slits today and the linen handkerchief that flowed down from his collar darkened the shadows beneath them.

"I gather you're doing a lot now," smiled Mister Lafkowitz, although she had not yet answered the question.

She looked at Mister Bilderbach. He turned away. His heavy shoulders pushed the door open wide so that the late afternoon sun came through the window of the studio and shafted yellow over the dusty living room. Behind her teacher she could see the squat long piano, the window, and the bust of Brahms.

"No," she said to Mister Lafkowitz, "I'm doing terribly." Her thin fingers flipped at the pages of her music. "I don't know what's the matter," she said, looking at Mister Bilderbach's stooped muscular back that stood tense and listening.

Mister Lafkowitz smiled. "There are times, I suppose, when one—"

A harsh chord sounded from the piano. "Don't you think we'd better get on with this?" asked Mister Bilderbach.

"Immediately," said Mister Lafkowitz, giving the bow one more scrape before starting toward the door. She could see him pick up his violin from the top of the piano. He caught her eye and lowered the instrument. "You've seen the picture of Heime?"

Her fingers curled tight over the sharp corner of the satchel. "What picture?"

"One of Heime in the *Musical Courier* there on the table. Inside the top cover."

The sonatina began. Discordant yet somehow simple. Empty but with a sharp-cut style of its own. She reached for the magazine and opened it.

There Heime was—in the left-hand corner. Holding his violin with his fingers hooked down over the strings for a pizzicato. With his dark serge knickers strapped neatly beneath his knees, a sweater and rolled collar. It was a bad picture. Although it was snapped in profile his eyes were cut around toward the photographer and his finger looked as though it would pluck the wrong string. He seemed suffering to turn around toward the picture-taking apparatus. He was thinner—his stomach did not poke out now—but he hadn't changed much in six months.

Heime Israelsky, talented young violinist, snapped while at work in his teacher's studio on Riverside Drive. Young Master Israelsky, who will soon celebrate his fifteenth birthday, has been invited to play the Beethoven Concerta with—

That morning, after she had practiced from six until eight, her dad had made her sit down at the table with the family for breakfast. She hated breakfast; it gave her a sick feeling afterward. She would rather wait and get four chocolate bars with her twenty cents lunch money and munch them during school—bringing up little morsels from her pocket under cover of her handkerchief, stopping dead when the silver paper rattled. But this morning her dad had put a fried egg on her plate and she had known that if it burst—so that the slimy yellow oozed over the white —she would cry. And that had happened. The same feeling was upon her now. Gingerly she laid the magazine back on the table and closed her eyes.

The music in the studio seemed to be urging violently and clumsily for something that was not to be had. After a moment her thoughts drew back from Heime and the concerta and the picture—and hovered around the lesson once more. She slid over on the sofa until she could see plainly into the studio—the two of them playing, peering at the notations on the piano, lustfully drawing out all that was there.

She could not forget the memory of Mister Bilderbach's

face as he had stared at her a moment ago. Her hands, still twitching unconsciously to the motions of the fugue, closed over her bony knees. Tired, she was. And with a circling, sinking away feeling like the one that often came to her just before she dropped off to sleep on the nights when she had over-practiced. Like those weary half-dreams that buzzed and carried her out into their own whirling space.

A *Wunderkind—a Wunderkind—a Wunderkind.* The syllables would come out rolling in the deep German way, roar against her ears and then fall to a murmur. Along with the faces circling, swelling out in distortion, diminishing to pale blobs—Mister Bilderbach, Mrs. Bilderbach, Heime, Mister Lafkowitz. Around and around in a circle revolving to the guttural *Wunderkind.* Mister Bilderbach looming large in the middle of the circle, his face urging —with the others around him.

Phrases of music seesawing crazily. Notes she had been practicing falling over each other like a handful of marbles dropped downstairs. Bach, Debussy, Prokofieff, Brahms— timed grotesquely to the far-off throb of her tired body and the buzzing circle.

Sometimes—when she had not worked more than three hours or had stayed out from high school—the dreams were not so confused. The music soared clearly in her mind and quick, precise little memories would come back—clear as the sissy "Age of Innocence" picture Heime had given her after their joint concert was over.

A *Wunderkind—a Wunderkind.* That was what Mister Bilderbach had called her when, at twelve, she first came to him. Older pupils had repeated the word.

Not that he had ever said the word to her. "Bienchen—"

(She had a plain American name but he never used it except when her mistakes were enormous.) "Bienchen," he would say, "I know it must be terrible. Carrying around all the time a head that thick. Poor Bienchen—"

Mister Bilderbach's father had been a Dutch violinist. His mother was from Prague. He had been born in this country and had spent his youth in Germany. So many times she wished she had not been born and brought up in just Cincinnati. How do you say *cheese* in German? Mister Bilderbach, what is Dutch for *I don't understand you?*

The first day she came to the studio. After she played the whole Second Hungarian Rhapsody from memory. The room graying with twilight. His face as he leaned over the piano.

"Now we begin all over," he said that first day. "It—playing music—is more than cleverness. If a twelve-year-old girl's fingers cover so many keys to a second—that means nothing."

He tapped his broad chest and his forehead with his stubby hand. "Here and here. You are old enough to understand that." He lighted a cigarette and gently blew the first exhalation above her head. "And work—work—work—. We will start now with these Bach Inventions and these little Schumann pieces." His hands moved again—this time to jerk the cord of the lamp behind her and point to the music. "I will show you how I wish this practiced. Listen carefully now."

She had been at the piano for almost three hours and was very tired. His deep voice sounded as though it had been straying inside her for a long time. She wanted to reach out and touch his muscle-flexed finger that pointed out the phrases, wanted to feel the gleaming gold band ring and the strong hairy back of his hand.

She had lessons Tuesday after school and on Saturday afternoons. Often she stayed, when the Saturday lesson was finished, for dinner, and then spent the night and took the streetcar home the next morning. Mrs. Bilderbach liked her in her calm, almost dumb way. She was much different from her husband. She was quiet and fat and slow. When she wasn't in the kitchen, cooking the rich dishes that both of them loved, she seemed to spend all her time in their bed upstairs, reading magazines or just looking with a half-smile at nothing. When they had married in Germany she had been a *lieder* singer. She didn't sing any more (she said it was her throat). When he would call her in from the kitchen to listen to a pupil she would always smile and say that it was *gut,* very *gut.*

When Frances was thirteen it came to her one day that the Bilderbachs had no children. It seemed strange. Once she had been back in the kitchen with Mrs. Bilderbach when he had come striding in from the studio, tense with anger at some pupil who had annoyed him. His wife stood stirring the thick soup until his hand groped out and rested on her shoulder. Then she turned—stood placid—while he folded his arms about her and buried his sharp face in the white, nerveless flesh of her neck. They stood that way without moving. And then his face jerked back suddenly, the anger diminished to a quiet inexpressiveness, and he had returned to the studio.

After she had started with Mister Bilderbach and didn't have time to see anything of the people at high school, Heime had been the only friend of her own age. He was

Mister Lafkowitz's pupil and would come with him to Mister Bilderbach's on evenings when she would be there. They would listen to their teachers' playing. And often they themselves went over chamber music together—Mozart sonatas or Bloch.

A *Wunderkind*—a *Wunderkind*.

Heime was a *Wunderkind*. He and she, then.

Heime had been playing the violin since he was four. He didn't have to go to school; Mister Lafkowitz's brother, who was crippled, used to teach him geometry and European history and French verbs in the afternoon. When he was thirteen he had as fine a technique as any violinist in Cincinnati—everyone said so. But playing the violin must be easier than the piano. She knew it must be.

Heime always seemed to smell of corduroy pants and the food he had eaten and rosin. Half the time, too, his hands were dirty around the knuckles and the cuffs of his shirts peeped out dingily from the sleeves of his sweater. She always watched his hands when he played—thin only at the joints with the hard little blobs of flesh bulging over the short-cut nails and the babyish-looking crease that showed so plainly in his bowing wrist.

In the dreams, as when she was awake, she could remember the concert only in a blur. She had not known it was unsuccessful for her until months after. True, the papers had praised Heime more than her. But he was much shorter than she. When they stood together on the stage he came only to her shoulders. And that made a difference with people, she knew. Also, there was the matter of the sonata they played together. The Bloch.

"No, no—I don't think that would be appropriate," Mister Bilderbach had said when the Bloch was suggested to end the programme. "Now that John Powell thing—the Sonate Virginianesque."

She hadn't understood then; she wanted it to be the Bloch as much as Mister Lafkowitz and Heime.

Mister Bilderbach had given in. Later, after the reviews had said she lacked the temperament for that type of music, after they called her playing thin and lacking in feeling, she felt cheated.

"That oie oie stuff," said Mister Bilderbach, crackling the newspapers at her. "Not for you, Bienchen. Leave all that to the Heimes and vitses and skys."

A *Wunderkind*. No matter what the papers said, that was what he had called her.

Why was it Heime had done so much better at the concert than she? At school sometimes, when she was supposed to be watching someone do a geometry problem on the blackboard, the question would twist knife-like inside her. She would worry about it in bed, and even sometimes when she was supposed to be concentrating at the piano. It wasn't just the Bloch and her not being Jewish—not entirely. It wasn't that Heime didn't have to go to school and had begun his training so early, either. It was—?

Once she thought she knew.

"Play the Fantasia and Fugue," Mister Bilderbach had demanded one evening a year ago—after he and Mister Lafkowitz had finished reading some music together.

The Bach, as she played, seemed to her well done. From the tail of her eye she could see the calm, pleased expression on Mister Bilderbach's face, see his hands rise climactically from the chair arms and then sink down loose and satisfied when the high points of the phrases had been passed successfully. She stood up from the piano when it was over, swallowing to loosen the bands that the music seemed to have drawn around her throat and chest. But—

"Frances—" Mister Lafkowitz had said then, suddenly, looking at her with his thin mouth curved and his eyes almost covered by their delicate lids. "Do you know how many children Bach had?"

She turned to him, puzzled. "A good many. Twenty some odd."

"Well then—" The corners of his smile etched themselves gently in his pale face. "He could not have been so cold—then."

Mister Bilderbach was not pleased; his guttural effulgence of German words had *Kind* in it somewhere. Mister Lafkowitz raised his eyebrows. She had caught the point easily enough, but she felt no deception in keeping her face blank and immature because that was the way Mister Bilderbach wanted her to look.

Yet such things had nothing to do with it. Nothing very much, at least, for she would grow older. Mister Bilderbach understood that, and even Mister Lafkowitz had not meant just what he said.

In the dreams Mister Bilderbach's face loomed out and contracted in the center of the whirling circle. The lip surging softly, the veins in his temples insisting.

But sometimes, before she slept, there were such clear memories; as when she pulled a hole in the heel of her stocking down, so that her shoe would hide it. "Bienchen,

Bienchen!" And bringing Mrs. Bilderbach's workbasket in and showing her how it should be darned and not gathered together in a lumpy heap.

And the time she graduated from Junior High.

"What you wear?" asked Mrs. Bilderbach the Sunday morning at breakfast when she told them about how they had practiced to march into the auditorium.

"An evening dress my cousin had last year."

"Ah—Bienchen!" he said, circling his warm coffee cup with his heavy hands, looking up at her with wrinkles around his laughing eyes. "I bet I know what Bienchen wants—"

He insisted. He would not believe her when she explained that she honestly didn't care at all.

"Like this, Anna," he said, pushing his napkin across the table and mincing to the other side of the room, swishing his hips, rolling up his eyes behind his horn-rimmed glasses.

The next Saturday afternoon, after her lessons, he took her to the department stores downtown. His thick fingers smoothed over the filmy nets and crackling taffetas that the saleswomen unwound from their bolts. He held colors to her face, cocking his head to one side, and selected pink. Shoes, he remembered too. He liked best some white kid pumps. They seemed a little like old ladies' shoes to her and the Red Cross label in the instep had a charity look. But it really didn't matter at all. When Mrs. Bilderbach began to cut out the dress and fit it to her with pins, he interrupted his lessons to stand by and suggest ruffles around the hips and neck and a fancy rosette on the shoulder. The music was coming along nicely then. Dresses and commencement and such made no difference.

Nothing mattered much except playing the music as it must be played, bringing out the thing that must be in her, practicing, practicing, playing so that Mister Bilderbach's face lost some of its urging look. Putting the thing into her music that Myra Hess had, and Yehudi Menuhin—even Heime!

What had begun to happen to her four months ago? The notes began springing out with a glib, dead intonation. Adolescence, she thought. Some kids played with promise —and worked and worked until, like her, the least little thing would start them crying, and worn out with trying to get the thing across—the longing thing they felt—something queer began to happen— But not she! She was like Heime. She had to be. She—

Once it was there for sure. And you didn't lose things like that. A *Wunderkind* . . . . A *Wunderkind*. . . . Of her he said it, rolling the words in the sure, deep German way. And in the dreams even deeper, more certain than ever. With his face looming out at her, and the longing phrases of music mixed in with the zooming, circling round, round, round—A *Wunderkind*. A *Wunderkind*. . . .

This afternoon Mister Bilderbach did not show Mister Lafkowitz to the front door, as he usually did. He stayed at the piano, softly pressing a solitary note. Listening, Frances watched the violinist wind his scarf about his pale throat.

"A good picture of Heime," she said, picking up her music. "I got a letter from him a couple of months ago—

telling about hearing Schnabel and Huberman and about Carnegie Hall and things to eat at the Russian Tea Room."

To put off going into the studio a moment longer she waited until Mister Lafkowitz was ready to leave and then stood behind him as he opened the door. The frosty cold outside cut into the room. It was growing late and the air was seeped with the pale yellow of winter twilight. When the door swung to on its hinges, the house seemed darker and more silent than ever before she had known it to be.

As she went into the studio Mister Bilderbach got up from the piano and silently watched her settle herself at the keyboard.

"Well, Bienchen," he said, "this afternoon we are going to begin all over. Start from scratch. Forget the last few months."

He looked as though he were trying to act a part in a movie. His solid body swayed from toe to heel, he rubbed his hands together, and even smiled in a satisfied, movie way. Then suddenly he thrust this manner brusquely aside. His heavy shoulders slouched and he began to run through the stack of music she had brought in. "The Bach —no, not yet," he murmured. "The Beethoven? Yes. The Variation Sonata. Opus 26."

The keys of the piano hemmed her in—stiff and white and dead-seeming.

"Wait a minute," he said. He stood in the curve of the piano, elbows propped, and looked at her. "Today I expect something from you. Now this sonata—it's the first Beethoven sonata you ever worked on. Every note is under control—technically—you have nothing to cope with but

the music. Only music now. That's all you think about."
He rustled through the pages of her volume until he
found the place. Then he pulled his teaching chair halfway
across the room, turned it around and seated himself, strad-
dling the back with his legs.

For some reason, she knew, this position of his usually
had a good effect on her performance. But today she felt
that she would notice him from the corner of her eye and
be disturbed. His back was stiffly tilted, his legs looked
tense. The heavy volume before him seemed to balance
dangerously on the chair back. "Now we begin," he said
with a peremptory dart of his eyes in her direction.

Her hands rounded over the keys and then sank down.
The first notes were too loud, the other phrases followed
dryly.

Arrestingly his hand rose up from the score. "Wait!
Think a minute what you're playing. How is this beginning
marked?"

"*An-andante.*"

"All right. Don't drag it into an *adagio* then. And play
deeply into the keys. Don't snatch it off shallowly that way.
A graceful, deep-toned *andante*—"

She tried again. Her hands seemed separate from the
music that was in her.

"Listen," he interrupted. "Which of these variations
dominates the whole?"

"The dirge," she answered.

"Then prepare for that. This is an *andante*—but it's not
salon stuff as you just played it. Start out softly, *piano*, and
make it swell out just before the arpeggio. Make it warm
and dramatic. And down here—where it's marked *dolce*

make the counter melody sing out. You know all that. We've gone over all that side of it before. Now play it. Feel it as Beethoven wrote it down. Feel that tragedy and restraint."

She could not stop looking at his hands. They seemed to rest tentatively on the music, ready to fly up as a stop signal as soon as she would begin, the gleaming flash of his ring calling her to halt. "Mister Bilderbach—maybe if I—if you let me play on through the first variation without stopping I could do better."

"I won't interrupt," he said.

Her pale face leaned over too close to the keys. She played through the first part, and, obeying a nod from him, began the second. There were no flaws that jarred on her, but the phrases shaped from her fingers before she had put into them the meaning that she felt.

When she had finished he looked up from the music and began to speak with dull bluntness: "I hardly heard those harmonic fillings in the right hand. And incidentally, this part was supposed to take on intensity, develop the foreshadowings that were supposed to be inherent in the first part. Go on with the next one, though."

She wanted to start it with subdued viciousness and progress to a feeling of deep, swollen sorrow. Her mind told her that. But her hands seemed to gum in the keys like limp macaroni and she could not imagine the music as it should be.

When the last note had stopped vibrating, he closed the book and deliberately got up from the chair. He was moving his lower jaw from side to side—and between his open lips she could glimpse the pink healthy lane to his throat and his strong, smoke-yellowed teeth. He laid the Beethoven gingerly on top of the rest of her music and propped his elbows on the smooth, black piano top once more. "No," he said simply, looking at her.

Her mouth began to quiver. "I can't help it. I—"

Suddenly he strained his lips into a smile. "Listen, Bienchen," he began in a new, forced voice. "You still play the Harmonious Blacksmith, don't you? I told you not to drop it from your repertoire."

"Yes," she said, "I practice it now and then."

His voice was the one he used for children. "It was among the first things we worked on together—remember. So strongly you used to play it—like a real blacksmith's daughter. You see, Bienchen, I know you so well—as if you were my own girl. I know what you have—I've heard you play so many things beautifully. You used to—"

He stopped in confusion and inhaled from his pulpy stub of cigarette. The smoke drowsed out from his pink lips and clung in a gray mist around her lank hair and childish forehead.

"Make it happy and simple," he said, switching on the lamp behind her and stepping back from the piano.

For a moment he stood just inside the bright circle the light made. Then impulsively he squatted down to the floor. "Vigorous," he said.

She could not stop looking at him, sitting on one heel with the other foot resting squarely before him for balance, the muscles of his strong thighs straining under the cloth of his trousers, his back straight, his elbows staunchly propped on his knees. "Simply now," he repeated with a gesture of his fleshy hands. "Think of the blacksmith—

working out in the sunshine all day. Working easily and undisturbed."

She could not look down at the piano. The light brightened the hairs on the backs of his outspread hands, made the lenses of his glasses glitter.

"All of it," he urged. "Now!"

She felt that the marrows of her bones were hollow and there was no blood left in her. Her heart that had been springing against her chest all afternoon felt suddenly dead. She saw it gray and limp and shriveled at the edges like an oyster.

His face seemed to throb out in space before her, come closer with the lurching motion in the veins of his temples. In retreat, she looked down at the piano. Her lips shook like jelly and a surge of noiseless tears made the white keys blur in a watery line. "I can't," she whispered. "I don't know why, but I just can't—can't any more."

His tense body slackened and, holding his hand to his side, he pulled himself up. She clutched her music and hurried past him.

Her coat. The mittens and galoshes. The schoolbooks and the satchel he had given her on her birthday. All from the silent room that was hers. Quickly—before he would have to speak.

As she passed through the vestibule she could not help but see his hands—held out from his body that leaned against the studio door, relaxed and purposeless. The door shut to firmly. Dragging her books and satchel she stumbled down the stone steps, turned in the wrong direction, and hurried down the street that had become confused with noise and bicycles and the games of other children.

DORIS LESSING

Notes for
a Case History

Maureen Watson was born at 93 Nelson's Way, N.1., in 1942. She did not remember the war, or rather, when people said "The War," she thought of Austerity: couponed curtains, traded clothes, the half pound of butter swapped for the quarter of tea. (Maureen's parents preferred tea to butter.) Further back, at the roots of her life, she *felt* a movement of fire and shadow, a leaping and a subsidence of light. She did not know whether this was a memory or a picture she had formed, perhaps from what her parents had told her of the night the bomb fell two streets from Nelson's Way and they had all stood among piles of smoking rubble for a day and night, watching firemen hose the flames. This feeling was not only of danger, but of fatality, of being helpless before great impersonal forces; and was how she most deeply felt, saw, or thought an early childhood which the social viewer would describe perhaps like this: "Maureen Watson, conceived by chance on an unexpected granted-at-the-last-minute leave, at the height of the worst war in history, infant support of a mother only occasionally upheld (the chances of war deciding) by a husband she had met in a bomb shelter during an air raid: poor baby, born into a historical upheaval which destroyed forty million and might very well have destroyed her."

As for Maureen, her memories and the reminiscences of her parents made her dismiss the whole business as boring, and nothing to do with her.

It was at her seventh birthday party she first made this clear. She wore a mauve organdy frock with a pink sash, and her golden hair was in ringlets. One of the mothers said: "This is the first unrationed party dress my Shirley has had. It's a shame, isn't it?" And her own mother said: "Well of course these war children don't know what they've missed." At which Maureen said: "*I* am not a war child." "What are you then, love?" said her mother, fondly exchanging glances.

"I'm Maureen," said Maureen.

"And I'm Shirley," said Shirley, joining cause.

Shirley Banner was Maureen's best friend. The Watsons and the Banners were better than the rest of the street. The Watsons lived in an end house, at higher weekly payments. The Banners had a sweets-paper-and-tobacco shop.

Maureen and Shirley remembered (or had they been told?) that once Nelson's Way was a curved terrace of houses. Then the ground-floor level had broken into shops: a grocer's, a laundry, a hardware, a baker, a dairy. It seemed as if every second family in the street ran a shop to supply certain defined needs of the other families. What other needs were there? Apparently none; for Maureen's parents applied for permission to the Council, and the ground floor of their house became a second grocery shop, by way of broken-down walls, new shelves, a deepfreeze. Maureen remembered two small rooms, each with flowered curtains where deep shadows moved and flickered from the two small fires that burned back to back in the centre wall that divided them. These two rooms disappeared in clouds of dust from which sweet-smelling planks of wood stuck out. Strange but friendly men paid her compliments on her golden corkscrews and asked her for kisses, which they did not get. They gave her sips of sweet tea from their canteens (filled twice a day by her mother) and made her bracelets of the spiralling fringes of yellow wood. Then they disappeared. There was the new shop. Maureen's Shop. Maureen went with her mother to the sign shop to arrange for these two words to be written in yellow paint on a blue ground.

Even without the name, Maureen would have known that the shop was connected with hopes for her future; and that her future was what her mother lived for.

She was pretty. She had always known it. Even where the shadows of fire and dark were, they had played over a pretty baby. "You were such a pretty baby, Maureen." And at the birthday parties: "Maureen's growing really pretty, Mrs. Watson." But all babies and little girls are pretty, she knew that well enough . . . no, it was something more. For Shirley was plump, dark—pretty. Yet their parents'—or rather, their mothers'—talk had made it clear from the start that Shirley was not in the same class as Maureen.

When Maureen was ten there was an episode of importance. The two mothers were in the room above Maureen's Shop and they were brushing their little girls' hair out. Shirley's mother said: "Maureen could do really well for herself, Mrs. Watson." And Mrs. Watson nodded, but sighed deeply. The sigh annoyed Maureen, because it contradicted the absolute certainty that she felt (it had been bred into her) about her future. Also because it had to do with the *boring* era which she remembered, or thought she did, as a tiger-striped movement of fire. *Chance:* Mrs. Watson's sigh was like a prayer to the gods of Luck: it was the sigh of a small helpless thing being tossed about by big seas and gales. Maureen made a decision, there and then, that she had nothing in common with the little people who were prepared to be helpless and tossed about. For she was going to be quite different. She was already different. Not only The War but the shadows of war had long gone, except for talk in the newspapers which had nothing to do with her. The shops were full of everything. The Banners' sweets-tobacco-paper shop had just been done up; and Maureen's was short of nothing. Maureen and Shirley, two pretty little girls in smart mother-made dresses, were children of plenty, and knew it, because their parents kept saying (apparently they did not care how tedious they were): "These kids don't lack for anything, do they? They don't know what it can be like, do they?" This, with the suggestion that they ought to be grateful for not lacking anything, always made the children sulky, and they went off to flirt their full many-petticoated skirts where the neighbours could see them and pay them compliments.

Eleven years. Twelve years. Already Shirley had subsided into her role of pretty girl's plainer girl friend, although of course she was not plain at all. Fair girl, dark girl, and Maureen by mysterious birthright was the "pretty one," and there was no doubt in either of their minds which girl the boys would try first for a date. Yet this balance was by no means as unfair as it seemed. Maureen, parrying and jesting on street corners, at bus stops, knew she was doing battle for two, because the boys she discarded Shirley got: Shirley got far more boys than she would have done without Maureen who, for her part, needed—more, *had* to have—a foil. Her role demanded one.

They both left school at fifteen, Maureen to work in the shop. She was keeping her eyes open: her mother's phrase. She wore a slim white overall, pinned her fair curls up, was neat and pretty in her movements. She smiled calmly when customers said: "My word, Mrs. Watson, your Maureen's turned out, hasn't she?"

About that time there was a second moment of consciousness. Mrs. Watson was finishing a new dress for Maureen, and the fitting was taking rather long. Maureen fidgeted and her mother said: "Well, it's your capital, isn't it? You've got to see that, love." And she added the deep unconscious sigh. Maureen said: "Well don't go on about it, it's not very nice, is it?" And what she meant was, not that the idea was not very nice, but that she had gone beyond needing to be reminded about it; she was feeling the irritated embarrassment of a child when it is reminded to clean its teeth after this habit has become second nature. Mrs. Watson saw and understood this, and sighed again; and this time it was the maternal sigh which means: "Oh dear, you are growing up fast! "Oh *Mum*," said Maureen, "sometimes you just make me tired, you do really."

Sixteen. She was managing her capital perfectly. Her assets were a slight delicate prettiness, and a dress sense that must have been a gift from God, or more probably because she had been reading the fashion magazines since practically before consciousness. Shirley had put in six months of beehive hair, pouting scarlet lips, and an air of sullen disdain; but Maureen's sense of herself was much finer. She modelled herself on film stars, but with an understanding of how far she could go—of what was allowable to Maureen. So the experience of being Bardot, Monroe, or whoever it was, refined her: she took from it an essence, which was learning to be a vehicle for other people's fantasies. So while Shirley had been a dozen stars, but really *been* them, in violent temporary transmogrifications, from which she emerged (often enough with a laugh) Shirley—plump, good-natured, and herself—Maureen remained herself through every role, but creating her appearance, like an altar ego, to meet the expression in people's eyes.

Round about sixteen, another incident: prophetic. Mrs. Watson had a cousin who worked in the dress trade, and this man, unthought-of for many years, was met at a wedding. He commented on Maureen, a vision in white gauze. Mrs. Watson worked secretly on this slender material for some weeks; then wrote to him: Could Maureen be a model? He had only remote connections with the world of expensive clothes and girls, but he dropped into the shop with frankly personal aims. Maureen in a white wrapper was still pretty, very; but her remote air told this shrewd man that she would certainly not go out with him. She was saving herself; he knew that air of self-esteem very well from other exemplars. Such girls do not go out with middle-aged cousins, except as a favour or to get something. However, he told Mrs. Watson that Maureen was definitely model material, but that she would have to do something about her voice. (He meant her accent of course; and so Mrs. Watson understood him.) He left addresses and advice, and Mrs. Watson was in a state of quivering ambition. She said so to Maureen: "This is your chance, girl. Take it." What Maureen heard was: "This is *my* chance."

Maureen, nothing if not alert for her Big Chance, for which her whole life had prepared her, accepted her mother's gift of a hundred pounds (she did not thank her, no thanks were due) and actually wrote to the school where she would be taught voice training.

Then she fell into sullen withdrawal, which she understood so little that a week had gone by before she said she must be sick—or something. She was rude to her mother: very rare, this. Her father chided her for it: even rarer. But he spoke in such a way that Maureen understood for the first time that this drive, this push, this family effort to gain her a glamorous future, came from her mother, her father was not implicated. For him, she was a pretty-enough girl, spoiled by a silly woman.

Maureen slowly understood she was not sick, she was growing up. For one thing: if she changed her "voice" so as to be good enough to mix with new people, she would no longer be part of this street, she would no longer be *Our*

Maureen. What would she be then? Her mother knew: she would marry a duke and be whisked off to Hollywood. Maureen examined her mother's ideas for her and shrank with humiliation. She was above all no fool, but she had been very foolish. For one thing: when she used her eyes, with the scales of illusion off them, she saw that the million streets of London blossomed with girls as pretty as she. What, then, had fed the illusion in herself and in other people? What accounted for the special tone, the special looks that always greeted her? Why, nothing more than that she, Maureen, because of her mother's will behind her, had carried herself from childhood as something special, apart, destined for a great future.

Meanwhile (as she clearly saw) she was in 93 Nelson's Way, serving behind the counter of Maureen's Shop. (She now wondered what the neighbours had thought—before they got used to it—about her mother's fondness so terribly displayed.) She was dependent on nothing less than that a duke or a film producer would walk in to buy a quarter of tea and some sliced bread.

Maureen sulked. So her father said. So her mother complained. Maureen was—thinking? Yes. But more, a wrong had been done her, she knew it, and the sulking was more of a protective silence while she grew a scab over a wound.

She emerged demanding that the hundred pounds should be spent on sending her to secretarial school. Her parents complained that she could have learned how to be a secretary for nothing if she had stayed on at school another year. She said: "Yes, but you didn't have the sense to make me, did you? What did you think—I was going to sell butter like you all my life?" Unfair, on the face of it; but deeply fair, in view of what they had done to her. In their different ways they knew it. (Mr. Watson knew in his heart, for instance, that he should never have allowed his wife to call the shop "Maureen's.") Maureen went, then, to secretarial school for a year. Shirley went with her: she had been selling cosmetics in the local branch of a big chain store. To raise the hundred pounds was difficult for Shirley's parents: the shop had done badly, had been bought by a big firm; her father was an assistant in it. For that matter, it wasn't all that easy for the Watsons: the hundred pounds was the result of small savings and pinchings over years.

This was the first time Maureen had thought of the word capital in connection with money, rather than her own natural assets: it was comparatively easy for the Watsons to raise money, because they had capital: the Banners had no capital. (Mrs. Watson said the Banners had had *bad luck*.) Maureen strengthened her will; and as a result the two families behaved even more as if the girls would have different futures—or, to put it another way, that while the two sums of a hundred pounds were the same, the Watsons could be expected to earn more on theirs than the Banners.

This was reflected directly in the two girls' discussions about boys. Shirley would say: "I'm more easygoing than you."

Maureen would reply: "*I* only let them go so far."

Their first decisions on this almighty subject had taken place years before, when they were thirteen. Even then Shirley went further ("let them go further") than Maureen. It was put down, between them, to Shirley's warmer temperament—charitably; for both knew it was because of Maureen's higher value in the market.

At the secretarial school they met boys they had not met before. Previously boys had been from the street or the neighbourhood, known from birth, and for this reason not often gone out with—that would have been boring (serious, with possibilities of marriage). Or boys picked up after dances or at the pictures. But now there were new boys met day after day in the school. Shirley went out with one for weeks, thought of getting engaged, changed her mind, went out with another. Maureen went out with a dozen, chosen carefully. She knew what she was doing—and scolded Shirley for being so *soft*. "You're just stupid, Shirl—I mean, you've got to get on. Why don't you do like me?"

What Maureen did was to allow herself to be courted, until she agreed at last, as a favour, to be taken out. First, lunch—a word she began to use now. She would agree to go out to lunch two or three times with one boy, while she was taken out to supper (dinner) by another. The dinner partner, having been rewarded by a closed-mouth kiss for eight, ten, twelve nights, got angry or sulky or reproachful, according to his nature. He dropped her, and the lunch partner was promoted to dinner partner.

Maureen ate free for the year of her training. It wasn't that she planned it like this: but when she heard other girls say they paid their way or liked to be independent, it seemed to Maureen wrongheaded. To pay for herself would be to let herself be undervalued: even the idea of it made her nervous and sulky.

At the end of the training Maureen got a job in a big architect's office. She was a junior typist. She stuck out for a professional office because the whole point of the training was to enable her to meet a better class of people. Of course she had already learned not to use the phrase, and when her mother did snubbed her with: "I don't know what you mean, better *class*, but it's not much point my going into that hardware stuck upstairs in an office by myself if I can get a job where there's some life about."

Shirley went into a draper's shop where there was one typist (female) and five male assistants.

In Maureen's place there were six architects, out most of the time, or invisible in large offices visited only by the real secretaries; a lower stratum of young men in training, designers, draftsmen, managers, etc., and a pool of typists.

The young men were mostly of her own class. For some months she ate and was entertained at their expense; and at each week's end there was a solemn ceremony, the high point of the week, certainly the most exciting moment in it, when she divided her wage. It was seven pounds (rising to ten in three years) and she allocated two pounds for clothes, four for the post office, and one pound for the week's odd expenses.

At the end of a year she understood two things. That she had saved something like two hundred pounds. That there was not a young man in the office who would take her out again. They regarded her, according to their natures, with resentment or with admiration for her cool management of them. But there was nothing doing *there*—so they all knew.

Maureen thought this over. If she were not taken out to meals and entertainment, she must pay for herself and save no money, or she must never go out at all. If she was going to be taken out, then she must give something in return. What she gave was an open mouth, and freedom to the waist. She calculated that because of her prettiness she could give much less than other girls.

She was using her *capital* with even more intelligence than before. A good part of her time—all not spent in the office or being taken out—went in front of her looking glass, or with the better-class fashion magazines. She studied them with formidable concentration. By now she knew she could have gone anywhere in these islands, except for her voice. Whereas, months before, she had sulked in a sort of fright at the idea of cutting herself off from her street and the neighbours, now she softened and shaped her voice, listening to the clients and the senior architects in the office. She knew her voice had changed when Shirley said: "You're talking nice, Maureen, much nicer than me."

There was a boy in the office who teased her about it. His name was Tony Head. He was in training to be an accountant for the firm, and was very much from her own background. After having taken her out twice to lunch, he had never asked her again. She knew why: he had told her. "Can't afford you, Maureen," he said. He earned not much more than she did. He was nineteen, ambitious, serious, and she liked him.

Then she was nineteen. Shirley was engaged to one of the assistants in her shop, and would be married next Christmas.

Maureen took forty pounds out of her savings and went on a tour to Italy. It was her first time out of England. She hated it: not Italy, but the fact that half the sixty people on the tour were girls, like herself, looking for a good time, and the other half elderly couples. In Rome, Pisa, Florence, Venice, the Italians mooned over Maureen, courted her with melting eyes, while she walked past them, distant as a starlet. They probably thought she was one. The courier, a sharp young man, took Maureen out to supper one night after he had finished his duties, and made it clear that her mouth, even if opened, and her breasts, were not enough. Maureen smiled at him sweetly through the rest of the trip. No one paid for her odd coffees, ices and drinks. On the last night of the trip, in a panic because the forty-pound investment had yielded so little, she went out with an Italian boy who spoke seven words of English. She thought him crude, and left him after an hour.

But she had learned a good deal for her forty pounds. Quietly, in her lunch hour, she went off to the National Gallery and to the Tate. There she looked, critical and respectful, at pictures, memorising their subjects, or main colours, learning names. When invited out, she asked to be taken to "foreign" films, and when she got back home wrote down the names of the director and the stars. She looked at the book page of the *Express* (she made her parents buy it instead of the *Mirror*) and sometimes bought a recommended book, if it was a best seller.

Twenty. Shirley was married and had a baby. Maureen saw little of her—both girls felt they had a new world of knowledge the other couldn't appreciate.

Maureen was earning ten pounds a week, and saved six.

There came to the office, as an apprentice architect, Stanley Hunt, from grammar school and technical college. Tallish, well-dressed, fair, with a small moustache. They took each other's measure, knowing they were the same kind. It was some weeks before he asked her out. She knew, by putting herself in his place, that he was looking for a wife with a little money or a house of her own, if he couldn't get a lady. (She smiled when she heard him using this word about one of the clients.) He tried to know clients socially, to be accepted by them as they accepted the senior architects. All this Maureen watched, her cool little face saying nothing.

One day, after he had invited a Miss Plast (Chelsea, well-off, investing money in houses) to coffee, and been turned down, he asked Maureen to join him in a sandwich lunch. Maureen thanked him delightfully, but said she already had an engagement. She went off to the National Gallery, sat on the steps, froze off wolves and pickups, and ate a sandwich by herself.

A week later, invited to lunch by Stanley, she suggested the Trattoria Siciliana which was more expensive, as she knew quite well, than he had expected. But this meal was a success. He was impressed with her, though he knew (how could he not, when his was similar?) her background.

She was careful to be engaged for two weeks. Then she agreed to go to the pictures—"a foreign film, if you don't mind, I think the American films are just boring." She did not offer to pay, but remarked casually that she had nearly six hundred pounds in the post office. "I'm thinking of buying a little business, sometime. A dress shop. I've got a cousin in the trade."

Stanley agreed that "with your taste" it would be a sure thing.

Maureen no longer went to the Palais, or similar places (though she certainly did not conceal from Stanley that she had "once"), but she loved to dance. Twice they went to the West End together and danced at a Club which was "a nice place." They danced well together. On the second occasion she offered to pay her share, for the first time in her life. He refused, as she had known he would, but she could see he liked her for offering: more, was relieved; in the office they said she was mean, and he must have heard them. On that night, taken home lingeringly, she opened her mouth for him and let his hands go down to her thighs. She felt a sharp sexuality which made her congratulate herself that she had never, like Shirley, gone "halfway" before. Well of course, girls were going to get married to just anybody if they let themselves be all worked up every time they were taken out!

But Stanley was not at all caught. He was too cool a customer, as she was. He was still looking for something better.

He would be an architect in a couple of years; he would be in a profession; he was putting down money for a house; he was good-looking, attractive to women, and with these assets he ought to do better than marry Maureen. Maureen agreed with him.

But meanwhile he took her out. She was careful often to be engaged elsewhere. She was careful always to be worth taking somewhere expensive. When he took her home, while she did not go so far as "nearly the whole way," she went "everything but"; and she was glad she did not like him better, because otherwise she would have been lost. She knew quite well she did not really like him, although her mind was clouded by her response to his hands, his moustache, his clothes and his new car.

She knew, because meanwhile a relationship she understood very well, and regretted, had grown up with Tony.

He, watching this duel between the well-matched pair, would grin and drop remarks at which Maureen coloured and turned coldly away. He often asked her out—but only for a "Dutch treat"—expecting her to refuse. "How's your savings account, Maureen? I can't save, you girls get it all spent on you." Tony took out a good many girls: Maureen kept a count of them. She hated him; yet she liked him, and knew she did. She relied on him above all for this grinning, honest understanding of her: he did not approve of her, but perhaps (she felt in her heart) he was right? During this period she several times burst into tears when alone, without apparent reason; afterwards she felt that life had no flavour. Her future was narrowing down to Stanley; and at these times she viewed it through Tony Head's eyes.

One night the firm had a party for the senior members of the staff. Stanley was senior, Maureen and Tony were not. Maureen knew that Stanley had previously asked another girl to go, and when he asked herself, was uncertain whether she could make it until the very last moment: particularly as his inviting her, a junior, meant that he was trying out on the senior members the idea of Maureen as a wife. But she acquitted herself very well. First, she was the best-looking woman in the room by far, and the best-dressed. Everyone looked at her and commented: they were used to her as a pretty typist; but tonight she was using all her will to make them look at her, to make her face and body reflect what they admired. She made no mistakes. When the party was over Stanley and two of the younger architects suggested they drive out to London airport for breakfast, and they did. The two other girls were middle-class. Maureen kept silent for the most part, smiling serenely. She had been to Italy, she remarked, when a plane rose to go to Italy. Yes, she had liked it, though she thought the Italians were too noisy; what she had enjoyed best was the Sistine Chapel and a boat trip on the Adriatic. She hadn't cared for Venice much, it was beautiful, but the canals smelled, and there were far too many people; perhaps it would be better to go in winter? She said all this, having a right to it, and it came off. As she spoke she remembered Tony, who had once met her on her way to the National Gallery. "Getting yourself an education, Maureen? That's right, it'll pay off well, that will."

She knew, thinking it all over afterwards, that the evening had been important for her with Stanley. Because of this, she did not go out with him for a week, she said she was busy talking to her cousin about the possibilities of a dress shop. She sat in her room thinking about Stanley, and when thoughts of Tony came into her mind, irritatedly pushed them away. If she could succeed with Stanley, why not with someone better? The two architects from that evening had eyed her all the following week: they did not, however, ask her out. She then found that both were engaged to marry the girls they had been with. It was bad luck: she was sure that otherwise they would have asked her out. How to meet more like them? Well, that was the trouble—the drive to the airport was a bit of a fluke; it was the first time she had actually met the seniors socially.

Meanwhile Stanley showed an impatience in his courtship—and for the first time. As for her, she was getting on for twenty-one, and all the girls she had grown up with were married and had their first or even their second babies.

She went out with Stanley to a dinner in the West End at an Italian restaurant. Afterwards they were both very passionate. Maureen, afterwards, was furious with herself: some borderline had been crossed (she supposed she still could be called a virgin?) and now decisions would have to be made. Stanley was in love with her. She was in love with Stanley. A week later he proposed to her. It was done with a violent moaning intensity that she knew was due to his conflicts over marrying her. She was not good enough. He was not good enough. They were second-best for each other. They writhed and moaned and bit in the car, and agreed to marry. Her eight hundred pounds would make it easier to buy the house in a good suburb. He would formally meet her parents next Sunday.

"So you're engaged to Stanley Hunt?" said Tony.

"Looks like it, doesn't it?"

"Caught him—good for you!"

"He's caught me, more like it!"

"Have it your way."

She was red and angry. He was serious.

"Come and have a bite?" he said. She went.

It was a small restaurant, full of office workers eating on luncheon vouchers. She ate fried plaice ("No chips, please") and he ate steak-and-kidney pudding. He joked, watched her, watched her intently, said finally: "Can't you do better than that?" He meant, and she knew it, better in the sense she would use herself, in her heart: he meant *nice*. Like himself. But did that mean that Tony thought *she* was nice? Unlike Stanley? She did not think she was, she was moved to tears (concealed) that he did. "What's wrong with him then?" she demanded, casual. "What's wrong with *you?* You need your head examined." He said it seriously, and they exchanged a long look. The two of them sat looking goodbye at each other: the extremely pretty girl at whom everyone in the room kept glancing and remarking on, and the good-looking, dark, rather fat young accountant who was brusque and solemn with disappointment in her. With love for her? Very likely.

She went home silent, thinking of Tony. When she thought of him she needed to cry. She also needed to hurt him.

But she told her parents she was engaged to Stanley, who would be an architect. They would have their own house, in (they thought) Hemel Hampstead. He owned a car. He was coming to tea on Sunday. Her mother forgot the dukes and the film producers before the announcement ended: her father listened judiciously, then congratulated her. He had been going to a football match on Sunday, but agreed, after persuasion, that this was a good-enough reason to stay home.

Her mother then began discussing, with deference to Maureen's superior knowledge, how to manage next Sunday to best advantage. For four days she went on about it. But she was talking to herself. Her husband listened, said nothing. And Maureen listened, critically, like her father. Mrs. Watson began clamouring for a definite opinion on what sort of cake to serve on Sunday. But Maureen had no opinion. She sat, quiet, looking at her mother, a largish ageing woman, her ex-fair hair dyed yellow, her flesh guttering. She was like an excited child, and it was not attractive. *Stupid, stupid, stupid*—that's all you are, thought Maureen.

As for Maureen, if anyone had made the comparison, she was "sulking" as she had before over being a model and having to be drilled out of her "voice." She said nothing but: "It'll be all right, Mum, don't get so worked up." Which was true, because Stanley knew what to expect; he knew why he had not been invited to meet her parents until properly hooked. He would have done the same in her place. He *was* doing the same: she was going to meet his parents the week after. What Mrs. Watson, Mr. Watson, wore on Sunday; whether sandwiches or cake were served; whether there were fresh or artificial flowers—none of it mattered. The Watsons were part of the bargain; what he was paying in return for publicly owning the most covetable woman anywhere they were likely to be; and for the right to sleep with her after the public display.

Meanwhile Maureen said not a word. She sat on her bed looking at nothing in particular. Once or twice she examined her face in the mirror, and even put cream on it. And she cut out a dress, but put it aside.

On Sunday Mrs. Watson laid tea for four, using her own judgement since Maureen was too deeply in love (so she told everyone) to notice such trifles. At four Stanley was expected, and at 3:55 Maureen descended to the living room. She wore: a faded pink dress from three summers before; her mother's cretonne overall used for housework; and a piece of cloth tied round her hair that might very well have been a duster. At any rate, it was a faded grey. She had put on a pair of her mother's old shoes. She could not be called plain; but she looked like her own faded elder sister, dressed for a hard day's spring cleaning.

Her father, knowledgeable, said nothing: he lowered the paper, examined her, let out a short laugh, and lifted it again. Mrs. Watson, understanding at last that this was a real crisis, burst into tears. Stanley arrived before Mrs Watson could stop herself crying. He nearly said to Mrs. Watson: "I didn't know Maureen had an older sister." Maureen sat listless at one end of the table; Mr. Watson sat grinning at the other, and Mrs. Watson sniffed and wiped her eyes between the two.

Maureen said: "Hello, Stanley, meet my father and mother." He shook their hands and stared at her. She did not meet his eyes: rather, the surface of her blue gaze met the furious, incredulous, hurt pounce of his glares at her. Maureen poured tea, offered him sandwiches and cake, and made conversation about the weather, and the prices of food, and the dangers of giving even good customers credit in the shop. He sat there, a well-set-up young man, with his brushed hair, his brushed moustache, his checked brown cloth jacket, and a face flaming with anger and affront. He said nothing but Maureen talked on, her voice trailing and cool. At five o'clock, Mrs. Watson again burst into tears, her whole body shaking, and Stanley brusquely left.

Mr. Watson said: "Well, why did you lead him on, then?" and turned on the television. Mrs. Watson went to lie down. Maureen, in her own room, took off the various items of her disguise, and returned them to her mother's room. "Don't cry, Mum. What are you carrying on like that for? What's the matter?" Then she dressed extremely carefully in a new white linen suit, brown shoes, beige blouse. She did her hair and her face, and sat looking at herself. The last two hours (or week) hit her, and her stomach hurt so that she doubled up. She cried; but the tears smeared her makeup, and she stopped herself with the side of a fist against her mouth.

It now seemed to her that for the last week she had simply not been Maureen; she had been someone else. What had she done it for? Why? Then she knew it was for Tony: during all that ridiculous scene at the table, she had imagined Tony looking on, grinning, but understanding her.

She now wiped her face quite clear of tears, and went quietly out of the house so as not to disturb her father and mother. There was a telephone booth at the corner. She stepped calm and aloof along the street, her mouth held (as it always was) in an almost smile. Bert from the grocer's shop said: "Hey, Maureen, that's a smasher. Who's it for?" And she gave him the smile and the toss of the head that went with the street and said: "You, Bert, it's all for you." She went to the telephone booth thinking of Tony. She felt as if he already knew what had happened. She would say: "Let's go and dance, Tony." He would say: "Where shall I meet you?" She dialled his number, and it rang and it rang and it rang. She stood holding the receiver, waiting. About ten minutes—more. Slowly she replaced it. *He had let her down.* He had been telling her, in words and without, to be something, to stay something, and now he did not care, he had let her down.

Maureen quietened herself and telephoned Stanley.

All right then, if that's how you want it, she said to Tony.

Stanley answered, and she said amiably: "Hello."

Silence. She could hear him breathing, fast. She could see his affonted face.

"Well, aren't you going to say anything?" She tried to make this casual, but she could hear the fear in her voice. Oh yes, she could lose him and probably had. To hide the fear she said: "Can't you take a joke, Stanley?" and laughed.

"A joke!"

She laughed. Not bad, it sounded all right.

"I thought you'd gone off your nut, clean off your rocker. . . ." He was breathing in and out, a rasping noise. She was reminded of his hot breathing down her neck and her arms. Her own breath quickened, even while she thought: I don't like him, I really don't like him at all . . . and she said softly: "Oh Stan, I was having a bit of a giggle, that's all."

Silence. Now, this was the crucial moment.

"Oh Stan, can't you see—I thought it was all just boring, that's all it was." She laughed again.

He said: "Nice for your parents, I don't think."

"Oh, they don't mind—they laughed after you'd left, though first they were cross." She added hastily, afraid he might think they were laughing at him: "They're used to me, that's all it is."

Another long silence. With all her will power she insisted that he should soften. But he said nothing, merely breathed in and out, into the receiver.

"Stanley, it was only a joke, you aren't really angry, are you, Stanley?" The tears sounded in her voice now, and she judged it better that they should.

He said, after hesitation. "Well, Maureen, I just didn't like it, I don't like that kind of thing, that's all." She allowed herself to go on crying, and after a while he said, forgiving her in a voice that was condescending and irritated: "Well, all right, all right, there's no point in crying, is there?"

He was annoyed with himself for giving in, she knew that, because she would have been. He had given her up, thrown her over, during the last couple of hours: he was pleased, really, that something from outside had forced him to give her up. Now he could be free for the something better that would turn up—someone who would not strike terror into him by an extraordinary performance like this afternoon's.

"Let's go off to the pictures, Stan. . . ."

Even now, he hesitated. Then he said, quick and reluctant: "I'll meet you at Leicester Square, outside the Odeon, at seven o'clock." He put down the receiver.

Usually he came to pick her up in the car from the corner of the street.

She stood smiling, the tears running down her face. She knew she was crying because of the loss of Tony, who had let her down. She walked back to her house to make up again, thinking that she was in Stanley's power now: there was no balance between them, the advantage was all his.

COLETTE

Green Sealing-wax

TRANSLATED BY ANTONIA WHITE

Round about fifteen, I was at the height of a mania for "desk-furniture." In this I was only imitating my father whose mania for it lasted in full force all his life. At the age when every kind of vice gets its claws into adolescence, like the hundred little hooks of a burr sticking into one's hair, a girl of fifteen runs plenty of risks. My glorious freedom exposed me to all of them and I believed it to be unbounded, unaware that Sido's maternal instinct, which disdained any form of spying, worked by flashes of intuition and leapt telepathically to the danger-point.

When I had just turned fifteen, Sido gave me a dazzling proof of her second sight. She guessed that a man above suspicion had designs on my little pointed face, the plaits that whipped against my calves and my well-made body. Having entrusted me to this man's family during the holidays, she received a warning as clear and shattering as the gift of sudden faith and she cursed herself for having sent me away to strangers. Promptly, she put on her little bonnet that tied under the chin, got into the clanking, jolting train—they were beginning to send antique coaches along a brand-new line—and found me in a garden, playing with two other little girls, under the eyes of a taciturn man, leaning on his elbow like the meditative Demon on the ledge of Notre-Dame.

Such a spectacle of peaceful family life could not deceive Sido. She noticed, moreover, that I looked prettier than I did at home. That is how girls blossom in the warmth of a man's desire, whether they are fifteen or thirty. There was no question of scolding me and Sido took me away with her without the irreproachably respectable man's having dared to ask her reason for her arrival or for our departure. In the train, she fell asleep before my eyes, worn out like someone who had won a battle. I remember that lunch-time went by and I complained of being hungry. Instead of flushing, looking at her watch, promising me my favourite delicacies—wholemeal bread, cream cheese and pink onions—all she did was to shrug her shoulders. Little did she care about my hunger-pangs, she had saved the most precious thing of all.

I had done nothing wrong, nor had I abetted this man, except by my torpor. But torpor is a far graver peril for a girl of fifteen than all the usual excited giggling and blushing and clumsy attempts at flirtation. Only a few men can induce that torpor from which girls awake to find themselves lost. That, so to speak, surgical intervention of Sido's cleared up all the confusion inside me and I had one of those relapses into childishness in which adolescence revels when it is simultaneously ashamed of itself and intoxicated by its own ego.

My father, a born writer, left few pages behind him. At the actual moment of writing, he dissipated his desire in material arrangements, setting out all the objects a writer needs and a number of superfluous ones as well. Because of him, I am not proof against this mania myself. As a result of having admired and coveted the perfect equipment of a writer's work-table, I am still exacting about the tools on my desk. Since adolescence does nothing by halves, I stole from my father's work-table, first a little mahogany setsquare that smelt like a cigar-box, then a white metal ruler. Not to mention the scolding, I received full in my face the glare of a small, blazing grey eye, the eye of a rival, so fierce that I did not risk it a third time. I confined myself to prowling, hungrily, with my mind full of evil thoughts, round all these treasures of stationery. A pad of virgin blotting-paper; an ebony ruler; one, two, four, six pencils, sharpened with a penknife and all of different colours; pens with medium nibs and fine nibs, pens with enormously broad nibs, drawing-pens no thicker than a blackbird's quill; sealing-wax, red, green and violet; a handblotter, a bottle of liquid glue, not to mention slabs of transparent amber-coloured stuff known as "mouth-glue"; the minute remains of a Spahi's cloak reduced to the dimensions of a pen-wiper with scalloped edges; a big inkpot flanked by a small ink-pot, both in bronze, and a lacquer bowl filled with a golden powder to dry the wet page; another bowl containing sealing-wafers of all colours (I used to eat the white ones); to right and left of the table, reams of paper, cream-laid, ruled, water-marked, and, of course, that little stamping-machine that bit into the white sheet, and, with one snap of its jaws, adorned it with an embossed name: *J.—J. Colette.* There was also a glass of water for washing paint-brushes, a box of water-colours, an address-book, the bottles of red, black and violet ink, the mahogany set-square, a pocket-case of mathematical instruments, the tobacco-jar, a pipe, the spirit-lamp for melting the sealing-wax.

A property owner tries to extend his domain; my father therefore tried to acclimatise adventitious subjects on his vast table. At one time there appeared on it a machine that could cut through a pile of a hundred sheets, and some frames filled with a white jelly on which you laid a written page face downwards and then, from this looking-glass original, pulled off blurred, sticky, anaemic copies. But my father soon wearied of such gadgets and the huge table returned to its serenity, to its classical style that was never disturbed by inspiration with its disorderly litter of crossed-out pages, cigarette-ends and "roughs" screwed up into paper balls. I have forgotten, heaven forgive me, the paper-knife section, three or four boxwood ones, one of imitation silver, and the last of yellowed ivory, cracked from end to end.

From the age of ten I had never stopped coveting those material goods, invented for the glory and convenience of a mental power, which come under the general heading of "desk-furniture." Children only delight in things they can hide. For a long time I secured possession of one wing, the left one, of the great four-doored double bookcase (it was eventually sold by order of the court). The doors of the upper part were glass-fronted, those of the lower, solid and made of beautiful figured mahogany. When you opened the lower left-hand door at a right angle, the flat touched the side of the chest-of-drawers, and, as the bookcase took up nearly the whole of one panelled wall, I would immure myself in a quadrangular nook formed by the side of the chest-of-drawers, the wall, the left section of the bookcase and its wide-open door. Sitting on a little footstool, I could gaze at the three mahogany shelves in front of me, on which were displayed the objects of my worship, ranging from cream-laid paper to a little cup of the golden powder. "She's a chip off the old block," Sido would say teasingly to my father. It was ironical that, equipped with every conceivable tool for writing, my father rarely committed himself to putting pen to paper, whereas Sido—sitting at any old table, pushing aside an invading cat, a basket of plums, a pile of linen, or else just putting a dictionary on her lap by way of a desk—Sido really did write. A hundred enchanting letters prove that she did. To continue a letter or finish it off, she would tear a page out of her household account book or write on the back of a bill.

She therefore despised our useless altars. But she did not discourage me from lavishing care on my desk and adorning it to amuse myself. She even showed anxiety when I explained that my little house was becoming too small for me. . . . "Too small. Yes, much too small," said the grey eyes. "Fifteen . . . Where is Pussy-Darling going, bursting out of her nook like a hermit-crab driven out of its borrowed shell by its own growth? Already, I've snatched her from the clutches of that man. Already, I've had to forbid her to go dancing on the 'Ring' on Low Sunday. Already. she's escaping and I shan't be able to follow her. Already. she wants a long dress and, if I give her one, the blindest will notice that she's a young girl. And if I refuse, everyone will look below the too-short skirt and stare at her woman's legs. Fifteen . . . How can I stop her from being fifteen, then sixteen, then seventeen years old?"

Sometimes, during that period, she would come and lean over the mahogany half-door that isolated me from the world. "What are you doing?" She could see perfectly well what I was doing but she could not understand it. I refused her the answer given her so generously by everything else she observed, the bee, the caterpillar, the hydrangea, the ice-plant. But at least she could see I was there, sheltered from danger. She indulged my mania. The lovely pieces of shiny coloured wrapping-paper were given me to bind my books and I made the gold string into book-markers. I had the first pen-holder sheathed in a glazed turquoise-coloured substance, with a moiré pattern on it, that appeared in Reumont's, the stationers.

One day my mother brought me a little stick of sealing-wax and I recognised the stub of green wax, the prize jewel of my father's desk. No doubt I considered the gift too overwhelming, for I gave no sign of ecstatic joy. I clutched the sealing-wax in my hand, and, as it grew warm, it gave out a slightly oriental fragrance of incense.

"It's very old sealing-wax," Sido told me, "and, as you can see, it's powdered with gold. Your father already had it when we were married; he'd been given it by his mother and his mother assured him that it was a stick of wax that had been used by Napoleon the First. But you've got to remember that my mother-in-law lied every time she opened her mouth, so ..."

"Is he giving it to me or have you taken it?"

Sido became impatient; she always turned irritable when she thought she was going to be forced to lie and was trying to avoid lying.

"When *will* you stop twisting a lock of hair around the end of your nose?" she cried. "You're doing your best to have a red nose with a blob at the tip like a cherry! That sealing-wax? Let's say your father's lending it to you and leave it at that. Of course, if you don't want ..."

My wild clutch of possession made Sido laugh again, and she said, with pretended lightness:

"If he wanted it, he'd ask you to give it back, of course!"

But he did not ask me to give it back. For a few months, gold-flecked green sealing-wax perfumed my narrow empire bounded by four mahogany walls, then my pleasure gradually diminished as do all pleasures to which no one disputes our right. Besides, my devotion to stationery temporarily waned in favour of a craze to be glamourous. I asserted my right to wear a "bustle," that is to say, I enlarged my small, round behind with a horsehair cushion which, of course, made my skirts much shorter at the back than in front. In our village, the frenzy of adolescence turned girls between thirteen and fifteen into madwomen who stole horsehair, cotton and wool, stuffed rags in a bag, and tied on the hideous contraption known as a "false bottom" on dark staircases, out of their mothers' sight. I also longed for a thick, frizzy fringe, leather belts so tight I could hardly breathe, high boned collars, violet scent on my handkerchief...

From that phase, I relapsed once more into childhood, for a feminine creature has to make several attempts before it finally hatches out. I revelled in being a Plain Jane, with my hair in pigtails and straight wisps straggling over my cheeks. I gladly renounced all my finery in favour of my old school pinafores with their pockets stuffed with nuts and string and chocolate. Paths edged with brambles, clumps of bullrushes, liquorice "shoe-laces," cats—in short, everything I still love to this day—became dear to me again. There are no words to hymn such times in one's life, no clear memories to illuminate them; looking back on them, I can only compare them to the depths of blissful sleep. The smell of haymaking sometimes brings them back to me, perhaps because, suddenly tired, as growing creatures are, I would drop for an hour into a dreamless sleep among the new-mown hay.

It was at this point there occurred the episode known for long afterwards as "the Hervouët will affair." Old Monsieur Hervouët died and no will could be found. The provinces have always been rich in fantastic figures. Somewhere, under old tiled roofs, yellow with lichen, in icy drawing-rooms and dining-rooms dedicated to eternal shade, on waxed floors strewn with death-traps of knitted rugs, in kitchen-garden paths between the hard-headed cabbages and the curly parsley, queer characters are always to be found. A little town or a village prides itself on possessing a mystery. My own village acknowledged placidly, even respectfully, the rights of young Gatreau to rave unmolested. This admirable example of a romantic madman, a wooden cigar between his lips, was always wildly tossing his streaming black curls and staring fixedly at young girls with his long, Arab eyes. A voluntary recluse used to nod good morning through a window-pane and passers would say of her admiringly:

"That makes twenty-two years since Madame Sibile left her room! My mother used to see her there, just as you see her now. And, you know, there's nothing the matter with her. In one way, it's a fine life!"

But Sido used to hurry her quick step and pull me along when we passed level with the aquarium that housed the lady who had not gone out for twenty-two years. Behind her clear glass pane the prisoner would be smiling. She always wore a linen cap; sometimes her little yellow hand held a cup. A sure instinct for what is horrible and prohibited made Sido turn away from that ground-floor window and that bobbing head. But the sadism of childhood made me ask her endless questions.

"How old do you think she is, Madame Sibile? At night does she sleep by the window in her armchair? Do they undress her? Do they wash her? And how does she go to the lavatory?"

Sido would start as if she had been stung.

"Be quiet. I forbid you to think about those things."

Monsieur Hervouët had never passed for one of those eccentrics to whom a market-town extends its slightly derisive protection. For sixty years he had been well-off and ill-dressed, first a "big catch" to marry, then a big catch married. Left a widower, he had remarried. His second wife was a former postmistress, thin and full of fire.

When she struck her breastbone, exclaiming "*That's where I can feel it burning!*" her Spanish eyes seemed to make the person she was talking to responsible for this unquenchable ardour. "I am not easily frightened," my father used to say, "but heaven preserve me from being left alone with Mademoiselle Matheix!"

After his second marriage, Monsieur Hervouët no longer appeared in public. As he never left his home, no one knew exactly when he developed the gastric trouble that was to carry him off. He was a man dressed, in all weathers, in black, including a cap with ear-flaps. Smothered in fleecy white hair and a beard like cotton-wool, he looked like an apple-tree attacked by woolly aphis. High walls and a gateway that was nearly always closed protected his second season of conjugal bliss. In summer a single rose-tree clothed three sides of his one-storeyed house and the thick fringe of wistaria on the crest of the wall provided food for the first bees. But we had never heard anyone say that Monsieur Hervouët was fond of flowers and, if we now and then caught sight of his black figure pacing to and fro under the pendants of the wistaria and the showering roses, he struck us as being neither responsible for nor interested in all this wealth of blossom.

When Mademoiselle Matheix became Madame Hervouët, the ex-postmistress lost none of her resemblance to a black-and-yellow wasp. With her sallow skin, her squeezed-in waist, her fine, inscrutable eyes and her mass of dark hair, touched with white and restrained in a knot on the nape of her neck, she showed no surprise at being promoted to middle-class luxury. She appeared to be fond of gardening. Sido, the impartial, thought it only fair to show some interest in her; she lent her books, and in exchange accepted cuttings and also roots of tree-violets whose flowers were almost black and whose stem grew naked out of the ground like the trunk of a tiny palm-tree. To me, Madame Hervouët-Matheix was an anything but sympathetic figure. I was vaguely scandalised that when making some assertions of irreproachable banality, she did so in a tone of passionate and plaintive supplication.

"What do you expect?" said my mother. "She's an old maid."

"But, Mamma, she's married!"

"Do you really imagine," retorted Sido acidly, "people stop being old maids for a little thing like that?"

One day, my father, returning from the daily "round of the town" by which this man who had lost one leg kept himself fit, said to my mother:

"A piece of news! The Hervouët relatives are attacking the widow."

"*No!*"

"And going all out for her, too! People are saying the grounds of the accusation are extremely serious."

"A new Lafarge case?"

"You're demanding a lot," said my father.

I thrust my sharp little mug between my two parents.

"What's that, the Lafarge case?"

"A horrible business between husband and wife. There's never been a period without one. A famous poisoning case."

"Ah!" I exclaimed excitedly. "What a piece of luck!"

Sido gave me a look that utterly renounced me.

"There you are," she muttered. "That's what they're all like at that age . . . A girl ought never to be fifteen."

"Sido, are you listening to me or not?" broke in my father. "The relatives, put up to it by a niece of Hervouët's, are claiming that Hervouët didn't die intestate and that his wife has destroyed the will."

"In that case," observed Sido, "you could bring an action against all widowers and all widows of intestates."

"No," retorted my father, "men who have children don't need to make a will. The flames of Hervouët's lady can only have scorched Hervouët from the waist up since . . ."

"Colette," my mother said to him severely, indicating me with a look.

"Well," my father went on. "So there she is in a nice pickle. Hervouët's niece says she saw the will, yes, saw it with her very own eyes. She can even describe it. A big envelope, five seals of green wax with gold flecks in it . . ."

"Fancy that!" I said innocently.

". . . and on the front of it, the instructions: 'To be opened after my death in the presence of my solicitor, Monsieur Hourblin or his successor.' "

"And suppose the niece is lying?" I ventured to ask.

"And suppose Hervouët changed his mind and destroyed his will?" suggested Sido. "He was perfectly free to do so, I presume?"

"There you go, the two of you! Already siding with the bull against the bullfighter!" cried my father.

"Exactly," said my mother. "Bullfighters are usually men with fat buttocks and that's enough to put me against them!"

"Let's get back to the point," said my father. "Hervouët's niece has a husband, a decidedly sinister gentleman by name of Pellepuits."

I soon got tired of listening. On the evidence of such words as "The relatives are attacking the widow!" I had hoped for bloodshed and foul play and all I heard was bits of gibberish such as "disposable portion of estate," "holograph will," "charge against X."

All the same my curiosity was reawakened when Monsieur Hervouët's widow paid us a call. Her little mantle of imitation Chantilly lace worn over hock-bottle shoulders, her black mittens from which protruded unusually thick, almost opaque nails, the luxuriance of her black-and-white hair, a big black taffeta pocket suspended from her belt that dangled over the skirt of her mourning, her "houri eyes," as she called them; all these details, that I seemed to be seeing for the first time, took on a new, sinister significance.

Sido received the widow graciously, took her into the garden and offered her a thimbleful of Frontignan and a wedge of home-made cake. The June afternoon buzzed over the garden, russet caterpillars dropped about us from the walnut-tree, not a cloud floated in the sky. My mother's pretty voice and Madame Hervouët's imploring one exchanged tranquil remarks; as usual, they talked about nothing but salpiglossis, gladiolus and the misdemeanours of servants. Then the visitor rose to go and my mother escorted her. "If you don't mind," said Madame Hervouët, "I'll come over in a day or two and borrow some books; I'm so lonely."

"Would you like to take them now?" suggested Sido.

"No, no, there's no hurry. Besides, I've noted down the titles of some adventure stories. Good-bye for the time being, and thank you."

As she said this, Madame Hervouët, instead of taking the path that led to the house, took the one that circled the lawn and walked twice round the plot of grass.

"Good gracious, whatever am I doing? Do forgive me."

She allowed herself a modest laugh and eventually reached the hall where she groped too high and to the left of the two sides of the folding door for a latch she had twenty times found on the right. My mother opened the front door for her and, out of politeness, stood for a moment at the top of the steps. We watched Madame Hervouët go off, keeping at first very close to the house, then crossing the road very hurriedly, picking up her skirts as if she were fording a river.

My mother shut the door again and saw that I had followed her.

"She is lost," she said.

"Who? Madame Hervouët? Why do you say that? How d'you mean, lost?"

Sido shrugged her shoulders.

"I've no idea. It's just my impression. Keep that to yourself."

I kept silence faithfully. This was all the easier as, continuing my series of metamorphoses like a grub, I had entered a new phase—the "enlightened bibliophile"—and I forgot Madame Hervouët in a grand turn-out of my stationery shop. A few days later, I was installing Jules Verne between *Les Fleurs Animées* and a relief atlas when Madame Hervouët appeared on the scene without the bell having warned me. For we left the front door open nearly all day so that our dog Domino could go in and out.

"How nice of a big girl like you to tidy up the bookshelves," exclaimed the visitor. "What books are you going to lend me today?"

When Madame Hervouët raised her voice, I clenched my teeth and screwed up my eyes very small.

"Jules Verne," she read, in a plaintive voice. "You can't read him twice. Once you know the secret, it's finished."

"There's Balzac up there, on the big shelves," I said, pointing to them.

"He's very heavy going," said Madame Hervouët.

Balzac, heavy going? Balzac, my cradle, my enchanted forest, my voyage of discovery? Amazed, I looked up at the tall black woman, a head taller than myself. She was toying with a cut rose and staring into space. Her features expressed nothing which could be remotely connected with opinions on literature. She became aware I was gazing at her and pretended to be interested in my writer's equipment.

"It's charming. What a splendid collection!"

Her mouth had grown older in the last week. She remained stooping over my relics, handling this one and that. Then she straightened herself up with a start.

"But isn't your dear mother anywhere about? I'd like to see her."

Only too glad to move, to get away from this "lost" lady, I rushed wildly out into the garden, calling "Mamma!" as if I were shouting "Fire!"

"She took a few books away with her," Sido told me when we were alone. "But I could positively swear she didn't even glance at their titles."

The rest of the "Hervouët affair" is linked, in my memory, with a vague general commotion, a kind of romantic blur. My clearest recollection of it comes to me through Sido, thanks to the extraordinary "presence" I still have of the sound of her voice. Her stories, her conversations with my father, the intolerant way she had of arguing and refuting, those are the things that riveted a sordid provincial drama in my mind.

One day, shortly after Madame Hervouët's last visit, the entire district was exclaiming "The will's been found!" and describing the big envelope with five seals that the widow had just deposited in Monsieur Hourblin's study. At once uneasy and triumphant, the Pellepuits-Hervouët couple and another lot, the Hervouët-Guillamats, appeared, along with the widow, at the lawyer's office. There, Madame Hervouët, all by herself, faced up to the solid, pitiless group, to what Sido called those "gaping, legacy-hunting sharks." "It seems," my mother said, telling the story, "that she smelt of brandy." At this point, my mother's voice is superseded by the hunchback's voice of Julia Vincent, a woman who went out ironing by the day and came to us once a week. For I don't know how many consecutive Fridays, I pressed Julia till I wrung out of her all she knew. The precise sound of that nasal voice, squeezed between the throat, the hump and the hollow, deformed chest, was a delight to me.

"The man as was most afeared was the lawyer. To begin with he's not a tall man, not half so tall as that woman. She, all dressed in black she was, and her veil falling down in front right to her feet. Then the lawyer picked up the envelope, big as that it was" (Julia unfolded one of my father's vast handkerchiefs) "and he passed it just as it was to the nephews so they could recognise the seals."

"But you weren't there, Julia, were you?"

"No, it was Monsieur Hourblin's junior clerk who was watching through the keyhole. One of the nephews said a word or two. Then Madame Hervouët stared at him like a duchess. The lawyer coughed, a-hem, a-hem, he broke the seals and he read it out."

In my recollection, it is sometimes Sido talking, sometimes some scandalmonger eager to gossip about the Hervouët affair. Sometimes it seems too that some illustrator, such as Bertall or Tony Johannot, has actually etched a picture for me of the tall, thin woman who never withdrew her Spanish eyes from the group of heirs-at-law and kept licking her lip to taste the *marc* brandy she had gulped down to give herself courage.

So Monsieur Hourblin read out the will. But, after the first lines, the document began to shake in his hands and he broke off, with an apology, to wipe his glasses. He resumed his reading and went right through to the end. Although the testator declared himself to be "sound in body and mind," the will was nothing but a tissue of absurdities, among others, the acknowledgement of a debt of two million francs contracted to Louise-Léonie-Alberte Matheix, beloved spouse of Clovis-Edme Hervouët.

The reading finished in silence and not one voice was raised from the block of silent heirs.

"It seems," said Sido, "that, after the reading, the silence was such you could hear the wasps buzzing in the vine-arbour outside the window. The Pellepuits and the various Guillamats did nothing but stare at Madame Hervouët, without stirring a finger. Why aren't cupidity and avarice possessed of second sight? It was a female Guillamat, less stupid than the others, who said afterwards that, before anyone had spoken, Madame Hervouët began to make peculiar movements with her neck, like a hen that's swallowed a hairy caterpillar.

The story of the last scene of that meeting spread like wildfire through the streets, through people's homes, through the cafés, through the fair-grounds. Monsieur Hourblin had been the first to speak above the vibrating hum of the wasps.

"On my soul and conscience, I find myself obliged to declare that the handwriting of the will does not correspond..."

A loud yelping interrupted him. Before him, before the heirs, there was no longer any Widow Hervouët, but a sombre Fury whirling round and stamping her feet, a kind of black dervish, lacerating herself, muttering and shrieking. To her admissions of forgery, the crazy woman added others, so rich in the names of vegetable poisons, such as buckthorn and hemlock, that the lawyer, in consternation, exclaimed naïvely:

"Stop, my poor good lady, you're telling us far more than anyone has asked you to!"

A lunatic asylum engulfed the madwoman and, if the

Hervouët affair persisted in some memories, at least, there was no "Hervouët case" at the assizes.

"Why, Mamma?" I asked.

"Mad people aren't tried. Or else they'd have to have judges who were mad too. That wouldn't be a bad idea, when you come to think of it..."

To pursue her train of thought better, she dropped the task with which her hands were busy; graceful hands that she took no care of. Perhaps, that particular day, she was shelling haricot beans. Or else, with her little finger stuck in the air, she was coating my father's crutch with black varnish...

"Yes, judges who would be able to assess the element of calculation in madness, who could sift out the hidden grain of lucidity, of deliberate fraud."

The moralist who was raining these unexpected conclusions on a fifteen-year-old head was encased in a blue gardener's apron, far too big for her, that made her look quite plump. Her grey gaze, terribly direct, fixed me now through her spectacles, now over the top of them. But in spite of the apron, the rolled-up sleeves, the sabots and the haricot beans, she never looked humble or common.

"What I do blame Madame Hervouët for," Sido went on, "is her megalomania. *Folie de grandeur* is the source of any number of crimes. Nothing exasperates me more than the imbecile who imagines he's capable of planning and executing a crime without being punished for it. Don't you agree it's Madame Hervouët's stupidity that makes her case so sickening? Poisoning poor old Hervouët with extremely bitter herbal concoctions, right, that wasn't difficult. Inept murderer, stupid victim, it's tit for tat. But to try and imitate a handwriting without having the slightest gift for forgery, to trust to a special, rare kind of sealing wax, what petty ruses, great heavens, what fatuous conceit!"

"But why did she confess?"

"Ah," said Sido reflectively. "That's because a confession is almost inevitable. A confession is like . . . let's see . . . yes . . . it's like a stranger you carry inside you . . ."

"Like a child?"

"No, not a child. With a child, you know the exact date it's going to leave you. Whereas a confession bursts out quite suddenly, just when you weren't expecting it, it tastes its liberty, it stretches its limbs. It shouts, it cuts capers. She accompanied hers with a dance, that poor murderess who thought herself so clever."

It shouts, it cuts capers . . . Just like that, then and there, my own secret burst out into Sido's ear: on the very day of Madame Hervouët's last visit I had noticed the disappearance of the little stick of green sealing-wax powdered with gold.

SHIRLEY ANN GRAU

Miss
Yellow Eyes

Pete brought Chris home one evening after supper. I remember it was early spring, because the Talisman rosebush by the kitchen steps had begun to blossom out. For that time of year it was cool: there was a good stiff wind off the river that shook the old bush and creaked it, knocked the biggest flowers to bits, and blew their petals into a little heap against the side of the wood steps. The Johnsons, who lived in the house next door, had put their bedspread out to air and forgot to take it in. So it was hanging out there on the porch railing, a pink spread with a fan-tailed yellow peacock in the middle. I could hear it flapping—loud when the wind was up, and very soft when it fell. And from out on the river there were the soft low tones of the ships' whistles. And I could hear a mockingbird too, perched up on top the house, singing away, forgetting that it was nighttime. And in all this, Pete's steps in the side alley, coming to the kitchen door.

"Hi, kid!" Pete held open the door with one arm stretched behind him. Chris came in.

I thought at first: that's a white man. And I wondered what a white man would do coming here. I got a second look and saw the difference, saw I'd made a mistake. His skin wasn't dark at all, but only sun-tanned. (Lots of white men were darker.) His eyes were a pale blue, the color of the china Ma got with the Octagon soap coupons. He had brown hair—no, it was closer to red, and only slightly wavy. He looked like a white man, almost. But I saw the difference. Maybe it was just his way of carrying himself—that was like a Negro.

But he was the handsomest man I'd ever seen, excepting none. I could feel the bottom of my stomach roll up into a hard ball.

"This here's Celia," Pete said.

Chris grinned and his blue eyes crinkled up into almost closed slits. He sat down at the table opposite me, flipping shut the book I'd been reading. "Evening's no time to be busy, kid."

Pete picked up the coffeepot from where it always stood on the back of the stove and shook it gently. "There's some here all right," he said to Chris as he reached up to the shelf for a couple of cups. "You want anything in yours? I reckon there'd be a can of milk in the icebox."

"No," Chris said. "I like it black."

Pete lit the fire under the speckled enamel coffeepot. "Where's Ma?"

"They having a dinner tonight . . . she said she'll be real late." Ma worked as a cook in one of the big houses on St. Charles Avenue. When there was a dinner, it meant she'd have to stay around and clean up afterwards and wouldn't get home till eleven or twelve maybe.

"She'll get tomorrow off, though," I told Chris.

"Good enough." He grinned and his teeth were very square and bright.

They sat down at the table with me and stretched out their legs. Holding the coffee cup to his mouth, Chris reached out one finger and rubbed the petals of the big yellow rose in the drinking glass in the center of the table. "That's real pretty."

"Lena's been putting them there," Pete said.

"That's sure the one I want to meet," Chris said, and grinned over at Pete, and I knew that he'd been talking about Lena.

She was the sort of girl you talk about, she was that beautiful—with light-brown hair that was shoulder-length and perfectly straight and ivory skin and eyes that were light brown with flecks of yellow in them. She was all gold-colored. Sometimes when she stood in the sun you could almost think the light was shining right through her.

She was near seventeen then, three years older than I was. The boys in high school all followed her around until the other girls hated her. Every chance they got they would play some mean trick on her, kicking dust in her lunch, or roughing her up playing basketball, or tearing pages out of her books. Lena hardly ever lost her temper; she didn't really seem to care. "I reckon I know who the boys are looking at," she told me. She was right. There was always a bunch of them trying to sit next to her in class or walk next to her down the hall. And when school was through, there was always a bunch of them waiting around the door, wanting to take her home, or for rides if they had cars. And when she finally came sauntering out, with her books tucked up under one arm, she wouldn't pay them much attention; she'd just give them a kind of little smile (to keep them from going to the other girls) and walk home by herself, with maybe a few of them trailing along behind. I used to wait and watch her leave and then I'd go home a different way. I didn't want to interfere.

But, for all that, she didn't go out very much. And never with the same boy for very long. Once Hoyt Carmichael came around and stood in the kitchen door, asking for her, just begging to see her. She wouldn't even come out to talk to him. Ma asked her later if there was something wrong and Lena just nodded and shrugged her shoulders all at once. Ma hugged her then and you could see the relief in her face; she worried so about Lena, about her being so very pretty.

Pete said: "You sure got to meet her, Chris, man."

And I said to Chris: "She's over by the Johnsons'." I got up and opened the door and yelled out into the alley: "Lena!"

She came in a few minutes. We could hear her steps on the alley bricks, slow. She never did hurry. Finally she opened the screen and stood there, looking from one to the other.

I said: "This is my sister, Magdalena."

"And this here is Chris Watkin," Pete said.

Chris had got up and bowed real solemnly. "I'm pleased to meet you."

Lena brushed the hair back from her forehead. She had long fingers, and hands so thin that the veins stood out blue on the backs. "Nobody calls me Magdalena," she said, "except Celia, now and then. Just Lena."

Chris's eyes crinkled up out of sight the way they had before. "I might could just call you Miss Yellow Eyes. Old Miss Yellow Eyes."

Lena just wrinkled her nose at him. In that light her eyes did look yellow, but usually if a man said something like that she'd walk out. Not this time. She just poured herself a cup of coffee, and when Chris pulled out a chair for her, she sat down, next to him.

I looked at them and I thought: they look like a white couple. And they did. Unless you had sharp trained eyes, like the people down here do, you would have thought they were white and you would have thought they made a handsome couple.

Chris looked over at me and lifted an eyebrow. Just one, the left one; it reached up high and arched in his forehead. "What you looking so solemn for, Celia?"

"Nothing."

And Lena asked: "You work with Pete at the railroad?"

"Sure," he said, and smiled at her. Only, more than his mouth was smiling. "We go swinging on and off those old tenders like hell afire. Jumping on and off those cars."

"I reckon that's hard work."

He laughed this time out loud. "I ain't exactly little." He bent forward and hunched his shoulders up a little so she could see the way the muscles swelled against the cloth of his shirt.

"You got fine shoulders, Mr. Watkin," she said. "I reckon they're even better than Pete there."

Pete grunted and finished his coffee. But she was right. Pete's shoulders were almost square out from his neck. Chris's weren't. They looked almost sloped and hunched the way flat bands of muscles reached up into his neck.

Chris shrugged and stood up. "Do you reckon you would like to walk around the corner for a couple of beers?"

"Okay," Pete said.

Lena lifted one eyebrow, just the way he had done. "Mr. Watkin, you do look like you celebrating something."

"I sure am," he said.

"What?" I asked.

"I plain tell you later, kid."

They must have been gone near two hours because Ma came home before they did. I'd fallen asleep. I'd just bent my head over for a minute to rest my eyes, and my forehead touched the soft pages of the book—*Treasure Island*. I'd got it from the library at school; it was dog-eared and smelled faintly of peanuts.

Ma was saying: "Lord, honey, why ain't you gone to bed?"

I lifted my head and rubbed my face until I could see Ma's figure in the doorway. "I'm waiting for them," I said.

Ma took off her coat and hung it up on the hook behind the door. "Who them?"

"Lena," I said, "and Pete. And Chris." I knew what she was going to say, so I answered first. "He's a friend of Pete, and Lena likes him."

Ma was frowning very slightly. "I plain wonder iffen he belong to that club."

"I don't know."

It was called the Better Days Club and the clubroom was the second floor of a little restaurant on Tulane Avenue. I'd never gone inside, though I had passed the place: a small wood building that had once been a house but now had a sign saying LEFTY'S RESTAURANT AND CAFÉ in green letters on a square piece of board that hung out over the sidewalk and creaked in the wind. And I'd seen something else too when I passed: another sign, a small one tucked into the right center corner of the screen door, a sign that said *"White* Entrance to *Rear."* If the police ever saw that they'd have found an excuse to raid the place and break up everything in it.

Ma kept asking Pete what they did there. Most time he didn't bother to answer. Once when she'd just insisted, he'd said, "We're fixing to have better times come." And sometimes he'd bring home little papers, not much more than book-size, with names like *New Day* and *Daily Sentinel* and *Watcher.*

Ma would burn the papers if she got hold of them. But she couldn't really stop Pete from going to the meetings.

She didn't try too hard because he was so good to her and gave her part of his pay check every week. With that money and what she made we always had enough. We didn't have to worry about eating, way some of our neighbors did.

Pete was a strange fellow—moody and restless and not happy. Sometimes—when he was sitting quiet, thinking or resting—there'd be a funny sort of look on his face (he was the darkest of us all): not hurt, not fear, not determination, but a mixture of all three.

Ma was still standing looking at me with a kind of puzzled expression on her face when we heard them, the three of them, coming home. They'd had a few beers and, what with the cold air outside, they all felt fine. They were singing too; I recognized the tune; it was the one from the jukebox around the corner in that bar.

Ma said: "They got no cause to be making a racket like that. Somebody might could call the police." Ma was terribly afraid of the police. She'd never had anything to do with them, but she was still afraid. Every time a police car passed in the street outside, she'd duck behind the curtain and peep out. And she'd walk clear around a block so she wouldn't come near one of the blue uniforms.

The three came in the kitchen door, Pete first and then Lena and Chris.

Pete had his arms full of beer cans; he let them all fall out on the table. "Man, I like to drop them sure."

"We brought some for you, Ma," Lena said.

"And Celia too," Chris added.

"It's plenty late," Ma said, looking hard at Chris.

"You don't have to work tomorrow," I said.

So we stayed up late. I don't know how late. Because the beer made me feel fine and sick all at once. First everything was swinging around inside my head and then the room too. Finally I figured how to handle it. I caught hold and let myself ride around on the big whooshing circles. There were times when I'd forget there was anybody else in the room, I'd swing so far away.

"Why, just you look at Celia there," Ma said, and everybody turned and watched me.

"You sure high, kid," Chris said.

"No, I'm not." I was careful to space the words, because I could tell by the way Ma had run hers together that she was feeling the beer too.

Pete had his guitar in his lap, flicking his fingers across the strings. "You an easy drunk." He was smiling, the way he seldom did. "Leastways you ain't gonna cost some man a lotta money getting you high."

"That absolutely and completely right." Ma bent forward, with her hands one on each knee, and the elbows sticking out, like a skinny football-player. "You plain got to watch that when boys come to take you out."

"They ain't gonna want to take me out."

"Why not, kid?" Chris had folded his arms on the tabletop and was leaning his chin on them. His face was flushed so that his eyes only looked bluer.

"Not after they see Lena." I lifted my eyes up from his and let them drop over where I knew Lena was sitting. I just had time to notice the way the electric light made her skin gold and her eyes gold and her hair too, so that she seemed all one blurry color. And then the whole world tipped over and I went skidding off—but feeling extra fine because Chris was sitting just a little bit away next to Lena and she was looking at him like she'd never looked at any body else before.

Next thing I knew, somebody was saying: "Celia, look." There was a photograph in front of me. A photograph of a young man, in a suit and tie, leaning back against a post, with his legs crossed, grinning at the camera.

I looked up. Ma was holding the photograph in front of me. It was in a wide silver-colored frame, with openwork, roses or flowers of some sort.

Pete began laughing. "Just you look at her," he said; "she don't even know her own daddy."

"I never seen that picture before," I said, loud as I could.

I'd never seen my daddy either. He was a steward on a United Fruit Lines ship, a real handsome man. He'd gone ashore at Antigua one day and forgot to come back.

"He looks mighty much like Chris," Ma said as she cleared a space on the shelf over between the windows. She put the picture there. And I knew then that she'd got it out from the bottom of a drawer somewhere, because this was a special occasion for her too.

"Chris," I said, remembering, "you never did tell us what you celebrating."

He had twisted sideways in his chair and had his arms wrapped around the back. "I going in the army."

Out of the corner of my eye I saw Pete staring at him, his mouth twisting and his face darkening.

Ma clucked her tongue against her teeth. "That a shame."

Chris grinned, his head cocked aside a little. "I got to leave tomorrow."

Pete swung back and forth on the two legs of his tilted chair. "Ain't good enough for nothing around here, but we good enough to put in the army and send off."

"Man"—Chris winked at him—"there ain't nothing you can do. And I plain reckon you gonna go next."

"No." Pete spoke the word so that it was almost a whistle.

"I'm a man, me," Chris said. "Can't run out on what I got to do." He tipped his head back and whistled a snatch of a little tune.

"I wouldn't like to go in the army," Lena said.

Chris went on whistling. Now we could recognize the song:

> *Yellow, yellow, yellow, yellow, yellow gal,*
> *Yellow, yellow, yellow, yellow, yellow gal,*
> *She's pretty and fine*
> *Is the yellow gal. . . .*

Lena tossed her head. "I wouldn't like to none."

Chris stopped whistling and laughed. "You plain sound like Pete here."

Pete's face all crinkled up with anger. I thought: he looks more like a Negro when he loses his temper; it makes his skin darker somehow.

"Nothing to laugh about," he said; "can't do nothing around here without people yelling nigger at you."

"Don't stay around here, man. You plain crazy to stay around here." Chris tilted back his chair and stared at the ceiling. "You plain crazy to stay a nigger. I done told you that."

Pete scowled at him and didn't answer.

Lena asked quickly: "Where you got to go?"

"Oregon." Chris was still staring at the ceiling and still smiling. "That where you cross over."

"You sure?"

Chris looked at her and smiled confidently. "Sure I'm sure."

Pete mumbled something under his breath that we didn't hear.

"I got a friend done it," Chris said. "Two years ago. He working out of Portland there, for the railroad. And he turn white."

Lena was resting her chin on her folded hands. "They don't look at you so close. Or anything?"

"No," Chris said. "I heard all about it. You can cross over if you want to."

"You going?" I asked.

"When I get done with the stretch in the army." He lowered his chair back to its four legs and stared out the little window, still smiling. "There's lots of jobs there for a railroad man."

Pete slammed the flat of his hand down against the table. Ma's eyes flew open like a door that's been kicked wide back. "I don't want to pretend I'm white," he said. "I ain't and I don't want to be. I reckon I want to be same as white and stay right here."

Ma murmured something under her breath and we all turned to look at her. Her eyes had dropped half-closed again and she had her hands folded across her stomach. Her mouth opened very slowly and this time she spoke loud enough for us all to hear. "Talking like that—you gonna do nothing but break you neck that way."

I got so sleepy then and so tired, all of a sudden, that I slipped sideways out of my chair. It was funny. I didn't notice I was slipping or moving until I was on the floor. Ma got hold of my arm and took me off to bed with her. And I didn't think to object. The last thing I saw was Lena staring at Chris with her long light-colored eyes. Chris with his handsome face and his reddish hair and his movements so quick they almost seemed jerky.

I thought it would be all right with them.

I was sick the whole next day from the beer; so sick I couldn't go to school. Ma shook her head and Pete laughed and Lena just smiled a little.

And Chris went off to the army, all right. It wasn't long before Lena had a picture from him. He'd written across the back: "Here I am a soldier." She stuck the picture in the frame of the mirror over her dresser.

That was the week Lena quit school. She came looking for me during lunch time. "I'm going home," she said.

"You can't do that."

She shook her head. "I had enough."

So she walked out of school and didn't ever go back. (She was old enough to do that.) She bought a paper on her way home and sat down and went through the classi-fied ads very carefully, looking for a job. It was three days before she found one she wanted: with some people who were going across the lake to Covington for the summer. Their regular city maid wouldn't go.

They took her on right away because they wanted to leave. She came back with a ten-dollar bill in her purse. "We got to leave in the morning," she said.

Ma didn't like it, her quitting school and leaving home, but she couldn't really stop her.

And Lena did want to go. She was practically jumping with excitement after she came back from the interview. "They got the most beautiful house," she said to Ma. "A lot prettier than where you work." And she told me: "They say the place over the lake is even prettier—even prettier."

I knew what she meant. I sometimes went to meet Ma at the house where she worked. I liked to. It was nice to be in the middle of fine things, even if they weren't yours.

"It'll be real nice working there," Lena said.

That next morning, when she had got her things together and closed the lid of the suitcase, she told me to go down to the grocery at the corner, where there was a phone, and call a taxi. They were going to pay for it, she said.

I reckon I was excited; so excited that I called the wrong cab. I just looked at the back cover of the phone book where there was a picture of a long orange-color cab and a number in big orange letters. I gave them the address, then went back to the house and sat down on the porch with Lena.

The orange cab turned at the corner and came down our street. The driver was hanging out the window looking for house numbers; there weren't any except for the Stevenses' across the way. Bill Stevens had painted his number with big whitewash letters on his front door. The cab hit a rut in the street and the driver's head smacked the window edge. He jerked his head back inside and jammed the gears into second. Then he saw us: Lena and me and the suitcase on the edge of the porch.

He let the car move along slow in second with that

heavy pulling sound and he watched us. As he got closer you could see that he was chewing on the corner of his lip. Still watching us, he went on slowly—right past the house. He said something once, but we were too far away to hear. Then he was down at the other corner, turning, and gone.

Lena stood and looked at me. She had on her best dress: a light-blue one with round pockets in front. Both her hands were stuffed into the pockets. There was a handkerchief in the left one; you could see her fingers twisting it.

White cabs didn't pick up colored people: I knew that. But I'd forgot and called the first number, a white number, a wrong number. Lena didn't say anything, just kept looking at me, with her hand holding the handkerchief inside her pocket. I turned and ran all the way down to the corner and called the right number, and a colored cab that was painted black with gold stripes across the hood came and Lena was gone for the next four months, the four months of the summer.

It could have been the same cab brought her back that had come for her: black with gold stripes. She had on the same dress too, the blue one with round pockets; the same suitcase too, but this time in it was a letter of recommendation and a roll of bills she'd saved, all hidden in the fancy organdy aprons they'd given her.

She said: "He wanted me to stay on through the winter, but she got scared for their boy." And she held her chin stiff and straight when she said that.

I understood why that woman wanted my sister Lena out of the house. There wasn't any boy or man either that wouldn't look at her twice. White or colored it didn't seem to make a difference, they all looked at her in the same way.

That was the only job Lena ever took. Because she hadn't been home more than a few days when Chris came back for her.

I remember how it was—early September and real foggy. It would close down every evening around seven and wouldn't lift until ten or ten thirty in the morning. All night long you could hear the foghorns and the whistles on the boats out on the river; and in the morning there'd be even more confusion when everybody tried to rush away from anchor. That Saturday morning Lena had taken a walk up to the levee to watch. Pete was just getting up. I could hear him in his room. Ma had left for work early. And me, I was scrubbing out the kitchen, the way I did every Saturday morning. That was when Chris came back.

He came around to the kitchen. I heard his steps in the alley—quickly coming, almost running. He came bursting in the door and almost slipped on the soapy floor. "Hi, kid," he said, took off his cap, and rubbed his hand over his reddish hair. "You working?"

"Looks like," I said.

He'd grown a mustache, a thin line. He stood for a moment chewing on his lip and the little hairs he had brushed so carefully into a line. Finally he said: "Where's everybody?"

"Lena went up on the levee to have a look at the river boats."

He grinned at me, flipped his cap back on, gave a kind of salute, and jumped down the two steps into the yard.

I sat back on my heels, picturing him and Lena in my mind and thinking what a fine couple they made. And the little picture of my father grinned down at me from the shelf by the window.

Pete called: "Seems like I heard Chris in there."

"He went off to look for Lena."

Pete came to the door; he was only half dressed and he was still holding up his pants with his one hand. He liked to sleep late Saturdays. "He might could have stayed to say hello."

"He wanted to see Lena, I reckon."

Pete grinned briefly and the grin faded into a yawn. "You ought to have let him look for her."

"Nuh-uh." I picked up the bar of soap and the scrubbing brush again. "I wanted them to get together, I reckon."

"Okay, kid," Pete said shortly, and turned back to his room. "You helped them out."

Chris and Lena came back after a while. They didn't say anything, but I noticed that Lena was kind of smiling like she was cuddling something to herself. And her eyes were so bright they looked light yellow, almost transparent.

Chris hung his army cap on the back of a chair and then sprawled down at the table. "You fixing to offer me anything to eat?"

"You can't be hungry this early in the morning," Lena said.

"Men are always hungry," I said. They both turned.

"You tell 'em, kid," Chris said. "You tell 'em for me."

"Let's us go to the beach," Lena said suddenly.

"Sure, honey," Chris said softly.

She wrinkled her nose at him and pretended she hadn't heard. "It's the last night before they close down everything for the winter."

"Okay—we gonna leave right now?"

"Crazy thing," Lena smiled. "Not in the morning. Let's us go right after supper."

"I got to stay here till then?"

"Not less you want to."

"Reckon I do," Chris said.

"You want to come, Celia?" Lena asked.

"Me?" I glanced over at Chris quickly. "Nuh-uh."

"Sure you do," Lena said. "You just come along."

And Chris lifted one eyebrow at me. "Come along," he said. "Iffen you don't mind going out with people old as me."

"Oh, no," I said. "Oh, no."

I never did figure out quite why Lena wanted me along that time. Maybe she didn't want to be alone with Chris because she didn't quite trust him yet. Or maybe she just wanted to be nice to me. I don't know. But I did go. I liked the beach. I liked to stare off across the lake and imagine I could see the shore on the other side, which of course I couldn't.

So I went with them, that evening after supper. It took us nearly an hour to get there—three changes of busses because it was exactly across town: the north end of the city. All the way, all along in the bus, Chris kept talking, telling stories.

"Man," he said, "that army sure is something—big—I never seen anything so big. Just in our little old camp there ain't a space of ground big enough to hold all the men, if they called them all out together. . . ."

We reached the end of one bus line. He put one hand on Lena's arm and the other on mine and helped us out the door. His hand was broad and hard on the palm and almost cool to the touch.

In the other bus we headed straight for the long seat across the back, so we could sit all three together. He sat in the middle and, leaning forward a little, rested both hands on his knees. Looking at him out the corner of my eye, I could see the flat broad strips of muscle in his neck, reaching up to under his chin. And once I caught Lena's eye, and I knew that on the other side she was watching too.

"All together like that," he said. "It gives you the funniest feeling—when you all marching together, so that you can't see away on either side, just men all together—it gives you a funny sort of feeling."

He turned to Lena and grinned; his bright square teeth flashed in the evening dusk. "I reckon you think that silly."

"No," she said quickly, and then corrected herself: "of course I never been in the army."

"Look there," I said. We were passing the white beach. Even as far away as the road where we were, we could smell the popcorn and the sweat and the faint salt tingle from the wind off the lake.

"It almost cool tonight," Lena said.

"You ain't gonna be cold?"

"You don't got to worry about me."

"I reckon I do," he said.

Lena shook her head, and her eyes had a soft holding look in them. And I wished I could take Chris aside and tell him that he'd said just the right thing.

Out on the concrete walks of the white beach, people

were jammed so close that there was hardly any space between. You could hear all the voices and the talking, murmuring at this distance. Then we were past the beach (the driver was going fast, grumbling under his breath that he was behind schedule), and the Ferris wheel was the only thing you could see, a circle of lights like a big star behind us. And on each side, open ground, low weeds, and no trees.

"There it is," Chris said, and pointed up through the window. I turned and looked and, sure enough, there it was; he was right: the lights, smaller maybe and dimmer, of Lincoln Beach, the colored beach.

"Lord," Lena said, "I haven't been out here in I don't know when. It's been that long."

We got off the bus; he dropped my arm but kept hold of Lena's. "You got to make this one night last all winter."

She didn't answer.

We had a fine time. I forgot that I was just tagging along and enjoyed myself much as any.

When we passed over by the shooting gallery Chris winked at Lena and me. "Which one of them dolls do you want?"

Lena wrinkled her nose. "I reckon you plain better see about getting 'em first."

He just shrugged. "You think I can do it, Celia?"

"Sure," I said. "Sure, sure you can."

"That's the girl for you," the man behind the counter said. "Thinks you can do anything."

"That my girl there all right." Chris reached in his pocket to pay the man. I could feel my ears getting red.

He picked up the rifle and slowly knocked down the

whole row of green and brown painted ducks. He kept right on until Lena and I each had a doll in a bright pink feather skirt and he had a purple wreath of flowers hung around his neck. By this time the man was scowling at him and a few people were standing around watching.

"That's enough, soldier," the man said. "This here is just for amateurs."

Chris shrugged. We all turned and walked away.

"You did that mighty well," Lena said, turning her baby doll around and around in her hands, staring at it.

"I see lots of fellows better."

"Where'd you learn to shoot like that?" I tugged on his sleeve.

"I didn't learn—"

"Fibber!" Lena tossed her head.

"You got to let me finish. Up in Calcasieu parish, my daddy, he put a shotgun in my hand and give me a pocket of shells. . . . I just keep shooting till I hit something or other."

It was hard to think of Chris having a father. "Where's he now?"

"My daddy? He been dead."

"You got a family?"

"No," Chris said. "Just me."

We walked out along the strip of sand, and the wind began pulling the feathers out of the dolls' skirts. I got out my handkerchief and tied it around my doll, but Lena just lifted hers up high in the air to see what the wind would do. Soon she just had a naked baby doll that was pink celluloid smeared with glue.

Lena and Chris found an old log and sat down. I went

wading. I didn't want to go back to where they were, because I knew that Chris wanted Lena alone. So I kept walking up and down in the water that came just a little over my ankles.

It was almost too cold for swimmers. I saw just one, about thirty yards out, swimming up and down slowly. I couldn't really see him, just the regular white splashes from his arms. I looked out across the lake, the way I liked to do. It was all dark now; there was no telling where the lower part of the sky stopped and the water began. It was all the one color, all of it, out beyond the swimmer and the breakwater on the left where the waves hit a shallow spot and turned white and foamy. Except for that, it was all the same dark until you lifted your eyes high up in the sky and saw the stars.

I don't know how long I stood there, with my head bent back far as it would go, looking at the stars, trying to remember the names for them that I had learned in school: names like Bear and Archer. I couldn't tell which was which. All I could see were stars, bright like they always were at the end of the summer and close; and every now and then one of them would fall.

I stood watching them, feeling the water move gently around my legs and curling my toes in the soft lake sand that was rippled by the waves. And trying to think up ways to stay away from those two who were sitting back up the beach, on a piece of driftwood, talking together.

Once the wind shifted a little suddenly or Chris spoke too loud, because I heard one word: "Oregon."

All of a sudden I knew that Lena was going to marry

him. Just for that she was going to marry him; because she wanted so much to be white.

And I wanted to tell Chris again, the way I had wanted to in the bus, that he'd said just the right thing.

After a while Lena stood up and called to me, saying it was late; so we went home. By the time we got there, Ma had come. On the table was a bag of food she had brought. And so we all sat around and ate the remains of the party: little cakes, thin and crispy and spicy and in fancy shapes; and little patties full of oysters that Ma ran in the oven to heat up; and little crackers spread with fishy-tasting stuff, like sugar grains only bigger, that Ma called caviar; and all sorts of little sandwiches.

It was one nice thing about the place Ma worked. They never did check the food. And it was fun for us, tasting the strange things.

All of a sudden Lena turned to me and said: "I reckon I want to see where Oregon is." She gave Chris a long look out of the corner of her eyes.

My mouth was full and for a moment I couldn't answer.

"You plain got to have a map in your schoolbooks."

I finally managed to swallow. "Sure I got one—if you want to see it."

I got my history book and unfolded the map of the whole country and put my finger down on the spot that said Oregon in pink letters. "There," I said; "that's Portland there."

Lena came and leaned over my shoulder; Pete didn't move; he sat with his chin in his hand and his elbows propped on the table.

"I want to stay here and be the same as white," he said, but we weren't listening to him.

Chris got out of the icebox the bottles of beer he had brought.

"Don't you want to see?" Lena asked him.

He grinned and took out his key chain, which had an opener on it, and began popping the caps off the bottles. "I looked at a map once. I know where it's at."

Ma was peering over my other shoulder. "It looks like it mighty far away."

"It ain't close," Chris said.

"You plain want to go there—" Ma was frowning at the map, straining to see without her glasses.

"Yes," Chris said, still popping the tops off bottles.

"And be white," Lena added very softly.

"Sure," Chris said. "No trouble at all to cross over."

"And you going there," Ma said again. She couldn't quite believe that anybody she was looking at right now could ever go that far away.

"Yea," Chris said, and put the last opened bottle with the others in a row on the table. "When I get out the army, we sure as hell going there."

"Who's we?" I asked.

"Lena and me."

Ma looked up at him so quickly that a hairpin tumbled out of her head and clicked down on the table.

"When we get married," he said.

Lena was looking at him, chewing her lower lip. "We going to do that?"

"Yea," he said. "Leastways if that what you want to do."

And Lena dropped her eyes down to the map again,

though I'd swear this time she didn't know what she was seeing. Or maybe everywhere she'd look she was seeing Chris. Maybe that was it. She was smiling very slightly to herself, with just the corners of her lips, and they were trembling.

They got married that week in St. Michel's Church. It was in the morning—nine-thirty, I remember—so the church was cold: biting empty cold. Even the two candles burning on the altar didn't look like they'd be warm. Though it only took a couple of minutes, my teeth were chattering so that I could hardly talk. Ma cried and Pete scowled and grinned by turns and Lena and Chris didn't seem to notice anything much.

The cold and the damp had made a bright strip of flush across Lena's cheeks. Old Mrs. Roberts, who lived next door, bent forward—she was sitting in the pew behind us —and tapped Ma on the shoulder. "I never seen her look prettier."

Lena had bought herself a new suit, with the money she'd earned over the summer: a cream-colored suit, with small black braiding on the cuffs and collar. She'd got a hat too, of the same color velvet. Cream was a good color for her; it was lighter than her skin somehow, so that it made her face stand out.

("She ought to always have clothes like that," Mayme Roberts said later, back at our house. She was old Mrs. Roberts's daughter, and seven kids had broken her up so that she wasn't even jealous of pretty girls any more. "Maybe Chris'll make enough money to let her have pretty clothes like that.")

Lena and Chris went away because he had to get back to camp. And for the first time since I could remember, I had a room all to myself. So I made Lena's bed all nice and careful and put the fancy spread that Ma had crocheted on it—the one we hardly ever used. And put the little pink celluloid doll in the middle.

Sometime after the wedding, I don't remember exactly when, Pete had an accident. He'd been out on a long run, all the way up to Abiline. It was a long hard job and by the time he got back to town he was dead tired, and so he got a little careless. In the switch yards he got his hand caught in a loose coupling.

He was in the hospital for two weeks or so, in the colored surgical ward on the second floor of a huge cement building that said Charity Hospital in carved letters over the big front door. Ma went to see him on Tuesdays and Saturdays and I just went on Saturdays. Walking over from the bus, we'd pass Lefty's Restaurant and Café. Ma would turn her head away so that she wouldn't see it.

One time, the first Saturday I went with Ma, we brought Pete a letter, his induction notice. He read it and started laughing and crying all at once—until the ward nurse got worried and called an intern and together they gave him a shot. Right up till he passed out, he kept laughing.

And I began to wonder if it had been an accident. . . .

After two weeks he came home. We hadn't expected him; we hadn't thought he was well enough to leave. Late one afternoon we heard steps in the side alley; Ma looked at me, quick and funny, and rushed over to open the door: it was Pete. He had come home alone on the streetcar and walked the three blocks from the car stop. By the time he got to the house he was ready to pass out: he had to sit down and rest his head on the table right there in the kitchen. But he'd held his arm careful so that it didn't start to bleed again. He'd always been afraid of blood.

Accidents like that happened a lot on the road. Maybe that was why the pay was so good. The fellows who sat around the grocery all day or the bar all had pensions because they'd lost an arm or a hand or a leg. It happened a lot; we knew that, but it didn't seem to make any difference.

Ma cried very softly to herself when she saw him so dizzy and weak he couldn't stand up. And I went out in the back yard, where he couldn't see, and was sick to my stomach.

He stayed in the house until he got some strength back and then he was out all day long. He left every morning just like he was working and he came back for dinner at night. Ma asked him once where he went, but he wouldn't say; and there was never any trouble about it. A check came from the railroad every month, regular; and he still gave Ma part of it.

Pete talked about his accident, though. It was all he'd talk about. "I seen my hand," he'd tell anybody who'd listen. "After they got it free, with the blood running down it, I seen it. And it wasn't cut off. My fingers was moving. I seen 'em. Was no call for them to go cut the hand off. There wasn't any call for them to do that, not even with all it hurting." (And it had hurt so bad that he'd passed out. They'd told us he just tumbled down all of a sudden —so that the cinders along the tracks cut in his cheek.)

He'd say: "Iffen it wasn't a man my color they wouldn't done it. They wouldn't go cut off a white man's hand."

He'd say: "It was only just one finger that was caught, they didn't have cause to take off the whole hand."

And when I heard him I couldn't help wondering. Wondering if maybe Pete hadn't tried to get one finger caught. The army wouldn't take a man with one finger missing. But just one finger gone wouldn't hamper a man much. The way Pete was acting wasn't like a man that had an accident he wasn't expecting. But like a man who'd got double-crossed somehow.

And looking at Ma, I could see that she was thinking the same thing.

Lena came home after a couple of months—Chris had been sent overseas.

She used to spend most of her days lying on the bed in our room, reading a magazine maybe, or writing to Chris, or just staring at the ceiling. When the winter sun came in through the window and fell on her, her skin turned gold and burning.

Since she slept so much during the days, often in the night she'd wake up and be lonesome. Then she'd call me. "Celia," she'd call real soft so that the sound wouldn't carry through the paperboard walls. "Celia, you awake?" And I'd tell her yes and wake up quick as I could.

Then she'd snap on the little lamp that Chris had given her for a wedding present. And she'd climb out of bed, wrapping one of the blankets around her because it was cold. And she'd sit on the cane-bottomed old chair and rock it slowly back and forth while she told me just what it would be like when Chris came back for her.

Sometimes Pete would hear us talking and would call: "Shut up in there." And Lena would only toss her head and say that he was an old grouch and not to pay any attention to him.

Pete had been in a terrible temper for weeks, the cold made his arm hurt so. He scarcely spoke any more. And he didn't bother going out after supper; instead he stayed in his room, sitting in a chair with his feet propped up on the windowsill, looking out where there wasn't anything to see. Once I'd peeped in through the half-opened door. He was standing in the middle of the room, at the foot of the bed, and he was looking at his stub arm, which was still bright-red-colored. His lips were drawn back tight against his teeth, and his eyes were almost closed, they were so squinted.

Things went on this way right through the first part of the winter. Chris was in Japan. He sent Lena a silk kimono —green, with a red dragon embroidered across the back. He didn't write much, and then it was just a line saying that he was fine. Along toward the middle of January, I think it was, one of the letters mentioned fighting. It wasn't so bad, he said; and it wasn't noisy at all. That's what he noticed most, it seemed: the quietness. From the other letters we could tell that he was at the front all the rest of the winter.

It was March by this time. And in New Orleans March is just rain, icy splashing rain. One afternoon I ran the dozen or so blocks home from school and all I wanted to do was sit down by the stove. I found Ma and Pete in the kitchen. Ma was standing by the table, looking down at the two yellow pieces of paper like she expected them to move.

The telegram was in the middle of the table—the folded paper and the folded yellow envelope. There wasn't anything else, not even the big salt-shaker which usually stood there.

Ma said: "Chris got himself hurt."

Pete was sitting across the room with his chair propped against the wall, tilting himself back and forth. "Ain't good enough for nothing around here," he said, and rubbed his stump arm with his good hand. "Ain't good enough for white people, but sure good enough to get killed."

"He ain't killed," Lena said from the next room. The walls were so thin she could hear every word. "He ain't got killed."

"Sure, Lena, honey," Ma said, and her voice was soft and comforting. "He going to be all right, him. Sure."

"Quit that," Ma told Pete in a fierce whisper. "You just quit that." She glanced over her shoulder toward Lena's room. "She got enough trouble without that you add to it."

Pete glared but didn't answer.

"You want me to get you something, Lena?" I started into our room. But her voice stopped me.

"No call for you to come in," she said.

Maybe she was crying, I don't know. Her voice didn't sound like it. Maybe she was though, crying for Chris. Nobody saw her.

Chris didn't send word to us. It was almost like he forgot. There was one letter from a friend of his in Japan, saying that he had seen him in a hospital there and that the nurses were a swell set of people and so were the doctors.

Lena left the letter open on the table for us all to see. That night she picked it up and put it in the drawer of her dresser with the yellow paper of the telegram.

And there wasn't anything else to do but wait.

No, there were two things, two things that Lena could do. The day after the telegram came, she asked me to come with her.

"Where?"

"St. Michel's." She was drying the dishes, putting them away in the cupboard, so I couldn't see her face, but I could tell from her voice how important this was.

"Sure," I said. "Sure, I'll come. Right away."

St. Michel's was a small church. I'd counted the pews once: there were just exactly twenty; and the side aisles were so narrow two people could hardly pass. The confessional was a single little recess on the right side in the back, behind the baptismal font. There was a light burning —Father Graziano would be back there.

"You wait for me," Lena said. And I sat down in the last pew while she walked over toward the light. I kept my head turned so that she wouldn't think I was watching her as she went up to the confessional and knocked very softly on the wood frame. Father Graziano stuck his gray old head out between the dark curtains. I didn't have to listen; I knew what Lena was asking him. She was asking him to pray for Chris. It only took her a minute; then she walked quickly up to the front, by the altar rail. I could hear her heels against the bare boards, each one a little explosion.

There were three or four candles burning already. She lit another one—I saw the circle of light get bigger as she put hers on the black iron rack.

"Let's go," she said; "let's go."

Father Graziano had come out of the confessional and was standing watching us. He was a small man, but heavy, with a big square head and a thick neck. He must have been a powerful man when he was young. Chris had a neck like that, muscled like that.

For a minute I thought he was going to come over and talk to us. He took one step, then stopped and rubbed his hand through his curly gray hair.

Lena didn't say anything until we reached the corner where we turned to go home. Without thinking, I turned.

"Not that way." She caught hold of my arm. "This way here." She went in the opposite direction.

I walked along with her, trying to see her face. But it was too dark and she had pulled the scarf high over her head.

"We got to go to Maam's," she said and her voice was muffled in the collar of her coat.

"To what?" not believing I'd heard her right.

"To Maam's."

Maam was a grisgris woman, so old nobody could remember when she'd been young or middle-aged even. Old as the river and wrinkled like it too, when the wind blows across.

She had a house on the *batture*, behind a clump of old thick hackberries. There was the story I'd heard: she had wanted a new house after a high water on the river had carried her old one away. (All this was fifty years ago, maybe.) So she'd walked down the levee to the nearest house, which was nearly a mile away: people didn't want to live close to her. She'd stood outside, looking out at the river and calling out: "I want a house. A fine new house. A nice new house. For me." She didn't say anything else, just turned and walked away. But the people inside had heard her and spread the word. Before they even began to fix the damage the flood had done to their own houses, the men worked on her house. In less than a week it was finished. They picked up their tools and left, and the next day they sent a kid down to spy and, sure enough, there was smoke coming out of the chimney. Maam had moved in: she must have been watching from somewhere close. Nobody knew where she had spent the week that she didn't have a house. And everybody was really too scared to find out.

She was still living in that house. It was built on good big solid pilings so that flood waters didn't touch it. I'd seen it once; Pete had taken me up on the levee there and pointed it out: a two-room house that the air and the river damp had turned black, on top a flat tin roof that shone in the sun. At the beginning of the dirt path that led down to the house I saw a little pile of food people had left for her: some white pieces of slab bacon, some tin cans. Pete wouldn't let me get close. "No sense fooling with things you don't understand," he said.

Maam didn't leave her house often. But when she did, when she came walking down the streets or along the levee, people got out of her way. Either they slipped down into the *batture* bushes and waited until she passed by on the top of the levee, or, in town, they got off the banquette and into the street when she came by—an old woman with black skin that was nearly gray and eyes hidden in the folds of wrinkles, an old woman wearing a black dress, and a red shawl over her head and shoulders, a bright red shawl with silver and black signs sewed onto it. And always she'd be staring at the girls; what she liked best was to be able to touch them, on the arm or the hand, or catch hold of a little piece of their clothes. That didn't happen often, everybody was so careful of her.

And still Lena had said: "We going to Maam's."

"Lord," I said, "why?"

"For Chris."

There wasn't anything I could answer to that.

It was still early, seven-thirty or eight, but nights don't seem to have time. The moon wasn't up yet; the sky was clear, with hard flecks of stars. Out on the river one ship was moving out—slipping between the riding lights of the other anchored ships that were waiting their turn at the docks below the point. You could hear the steady sound of the engines.

On top the levee the river wind was strong and cold and heavy-wet. I shivered even with a coat and scarf. There was a heavy frost like mold on the riverside slant of the levee. I stopped and pulled a clover and touched it to my lips and felt the sting of ice.

There was a light in Maam's house. We saw that as we came down the narrow little path through the hackberry bushes, the way that Pete wouldn't let me go when I was little. She must have heard us coming—walking is noisy on a quiet night—because without our knocking Maam opened the door.

I never did see her face. She had the red scarf tied high around her head so that it stuck out far on the sides. She mightn't have had a face, for all I could tell. The house was warm, very warm; I could feel the heat rush out all around her. She was wearing a black dress without sleeves, of some light material with a sheen like satin. She had tied a green cord tight around her middle. Under it her stomach stuck out like a pregnant woman's.

"I came to fetch something," Lena said. Her voice was tight and hard.

Inside the house a round spot was shining on the far wall. I stared at it hard: a tray, a round tin tray, nailed to the wall. I couldn't see more than that because there wasn't much light; just a single kerosene lamp standing in the middle of the room, on the floor. Being low like that, it made the shadows go upward on the walls so that even familiar things looked strange.

"I came to fetch something," Lena said. "For somebody that's sick."

Maam didn't move.

"To make him well," Lena added.

Maam turned around, made a circle back through her cabin, ending up behind her half-open door, where we couldn't see. I suppose we could have stepped inside and watched her—but we didn't. And in a couple of seconds she was back at the doorway. She was holding both arms straight down against her sides, the hands clenched. And she kept looking from Lena to me and back again.

Lena took her left hand out of her coat pocket and I

could see that she was holding a bill and a couple of coins. She moved them slowly back and forth; Maam's eyes followed but she did not move.

"You got to give it to me," Lena said. Her voice was high-pitched and rasping. I hadn't known it could be as rough as that.

Maam held out her hand: a thin black arm, all the muscles and tendons showing along the bone. She held out her arm, palm down, fist clenched. Then slowly, so that the old muscles under the thin skin moved in twisting lines, she turned the arm and opened the fingers. And in the palm there was a small bundle of cloth, white cloth. As we stared at it the three edges of the cloth, which had been pressed down in her hand, popped up slowly until they stuck straight up.

Lena reached out her right hand and took the three pointed edges of the cloth while her other hand dropped the money in its place. I could see how careful she was being not to touch the old woman.

Then we turned and almost ran back up the path to the top of the levee. I turned once near the top and looked back. Maam was still standing in the door, in her thin black sleeveless dress. She seemed to be singing something; I couldn't make out the words, just the sound. As she stood there, the lamplight all yellow behind her, I could feel her eyes reach out after us.

Lena had done all she could. She'd gone to the church and she'd prayed and lit a candle and asked the priest for special prayers. And she'd gone to the voodoo woman. She'd done all she could. Now there wasn't anything to do but wait.

You could see how hard waiting was for her. Her face was always thin, a little long, with fine features. And now you could almost see the strain lines run down her cheeks. The skin under her eyes turned blue; she wasn't sleeping. I knew that. She always lay very quiet in her bed, never tossing or turning. And that was just how I knew she was awake. Nobody lies stiff and still like that if they're really asleep; and their breathing isn't so shallow and quick.

I'd lie awake and listen to her pretending that she was asleep. And I'd want to get up and go over there and comfort her somehow. Only, some people you can't comfort. You can only go along with their pretending and pretend yourself.

That's what I did. I made out I didn't notice anything. Not the circles under her eyes; not the way she had of blinking rapidly (her eyes were so dry they burned); not the little zigzag vein that stood out blue on her left forehead.

One night we had left the shade up. There was a full moon, so bright that I woke up. Lena was really asleep then. I looked over at her: the light hadn't reached more than the side of her bed; it only reached her hand that was dangling over the edge of the bed, the fingers limp and curled a little. A hand so thin that the moonlight was like an X-ray, showing the bones.

And I wanted to cry for her if she couldn't cry for herself. But I only got up and pulled down the shade, and made the room all dark so I couldn't see any more.

Chris died. The word came one Thursday late afternoon. Ma was out sweeping off the front steps and she took the telegram from the boy and brought it to Lena. Her hand was trembling when she held it out. Lena's thin hand didn't move even a little bit.

Lena opened the envelope with her fingernail, read it, cleared the kitchen table, and put it out there. (We didn't need to read it.)

She didn't make a sound. She didn't even catch her breath. Her face didn't change, her thin, tired face, with the deep circles under the eyes and the strain lines down the cheeks. Only there was a little pulse began to beat in the vein on her forehead—and her eyes changed, the light eyes with flecks of gold in them. They turned one color: dark, dull brown.

She put the telegram in the middle of the table. Her fingers let loose of it very slowly. Their tips brushed back and forth on the edges of the paper a couple of times before she dropped her arm to her side and very slowly turned and walked into the bedroom, her heels sounding on the floor, slow and steady. The bed creaked as she sat down on it.

Ma had been backing away from the telegram, the corner of her mouth twitching. She bumped into a chair and she looked down—surprised at its being there, even. Then, like a wall that's all of a sudden collapsing, she sat down and bent her head in her lap. She began to cry, not making a sound, her shoulders moving up and down.

Pete was balancing himself on his heels, teetering back and forth, grinning at the telegram like it was a person.

I never saw his face look like that before; I was almost afraid of him. And he was Pete, my brother.

He reached down and flicked the paper edge with his fingers. "Good enough to die," he said. "We good enough to die."

There was a prickling all over me, even in my hair. I reckon I was shivering.

I tried to think of Chris dead. Chris shot. Chris in the hospital. Lying on a bed, and dead. Not moving. Chris, who was always moving. Chris, who was so handsome.

I stood and looked at the yellow telegram and tried to think what it would be like. Now, for Chris. I thought of things I had seen dead: dogs and mice and cats. They were born dead, or they died because they were old. Or they died because they were killed. I had seen them with their heads pulled aside and their insides spilled out red on the ground. It wouldn't be so different for a man.

But Chris . . .

"Even if you black," Pete was saying, "you good enough to get sent off to die."

And Ma said: "You shut you mouth!" She'd lifted her head up from her lap, and the creases on her cheeks were quivering and her brown eyes stared—cotton eyes, the kids used to call them.

"You shut you mouth!" Ma shouted. She'd never talked that way before. Not to Pete. Her voice was hoarser even, because she had been crying without tears.

And Pete yelled right back, the way he'd never done before: "Sweet Jesus, I ain't gonna shut up for nobody when I'm talking the truth."

I made a wide circle around him and went in the bedroom. Lena was sitting there, on the bed, with the pillows propped behind her. Her face was quiet and dull. There wasn't anything moving on it, not a line. There was no way of telling if she even heard the voices over in the kitchen.

I stood at the foot of the bed and put both hands on the cold iron railing. "Lena," I said, "you all right?"

She heard me. She shifted her eyes slowly over to me until they were looking directly at me. But she didn't answer. Her eyes, brown now and dark, stared straight into mine without shifting or moving or blinking or lightening. I stepped aside. The eyes didn't move with me. They stayed where they were, caught up in the air.

From the kitchen I could hear Pete and Ma shouting back and forth at each other until Ma finally gave way in deep dry sobbings that slowed and finally stopped. For a second or so everything was perfectly still. Then Ma said what had been in the back of our minds for months, only I didn't ever expect to hear her say it, not to her only boy.

"You no son of mine." She paused for a minute and I could hear the deep catching breath she took. "You no man even." Her voice was level and steady. Only, after every couple of words she'd have to stop for breath. "You a coward. A god-damn coward. And you made yourself a cripple for all you life."

All of a sudden Pete began to laugh—high and thin and ragged. "Maybe—maybe. But me, I'm breathing. And he ain't. . . . Chris was fine and he ain't breathing."

Lena didn't give any sign that she'd heard. I went around

to the side of the bed and took her hand: it was cold and heavy.

Pete was giggling; you could hardly understand what he was saying. "He want to cross over, him."

Ma wasn't interrupting him now. He went right ahead, choking on the words. "Chris boy, you fine and you brave and you ain't run out on what you got to do. And you ain't breathing neither. But you a man...."

Lena's hand moved ever so slightly.

"Lena," I said, "you all right?"

"Chris boy ... you want to cross over ... and you sure enough cross over ... why, man, you sure cross over ... but good, you cross over."

"Lena," I said, "don't you pay any mind to him. He's sort of crazy."

In the kitchen Pete was saying: "Chris, you a man, sure ... sure ... you sure cross over ... but ain't you gonna come back for Lena? Ain't you coming back to get her?"

I looked down and saw that my hand was shaking. My whole body was. It had started at my legs and come upward. I couldn't see clearly either. Edges of things blurred together. Only one thing I saw clear: Chris lying still and dead.

"It didn't get you nowhere, Chris boy," Pete was giggling. "Being white and fine, where it got you? Where it got you? Dead and rotten."

And Lena said: "Stop him, Chris."

She said: "Stop him, Chris, please."

I heard her voice, soft and low and pleading, the way she wouldn't speak to anyone else, but only her husband.

Chris, dead on the other side of the world, covered with ground.

Pete was laughing. "Dead and gone, boy. Dead and gone."

"Stop him, Chris," Lena said, talking to somebody buried on the other side of the world. "Stop him, Chris."

But I was the only one who heard her. Just me; just me.

You could see her come back from wherever she'd been. Her eyes blinked a couple of times slowly and when they looked at me, they saw me. Really saw me, her little sister. Not Chris, just Celia.

Slowly she pushed herself up from the bed and went into the kitchen, where Pete was still laughing.

Ma was sitting at the table, arms stretched out, head resting on them. She wasn't crying any more; it hardly looked like she was breathing.

"Dead and gone, man." Pete was teetering his chair back and forth, tapping it against the wall, so that everything on the little shelf over his head shook and moved. He had his mouth wide open, so wide that his eyes closed.

Lena hit him, hard as she could with the flat of her hand, hit him right across the face. And then she brought her left hand up, remembering to make a fist this time. It caught him square in the chest.

I heard him gasp; then he was standing up and things were falling from the shelf overhead. Lena stumbled back. And right where her hand struck the floor was the picture of our father, the picture in the silver metal frame, the one Ma had got out the night Chris first came.

She had it in her hand when she scrambled back to her feet. She was crying now, because he was still laughing.

From far away I could hear her gasping: "Damn, damn, damn, damn." And she swung the picture frame in a wide arc at his laughing mouth. He saw it coming and forgot for just a moment and lifted his arm to cover his face. And the frame and glass smashed into his stub arm.

He screamed: not loud, just a kind of high-pitched gasp. And he turned and ran. I was in the way and he knocked me aside as he yanked open the door. He missed his footing on the steps and fell down into the alley. I could hear him out there, still screaming softly to himself with the pain: "Jesus, Jesus, Jesus, Jesus."

Lena stood in the middle of the room, her hands hanging down empty at her sides. Her lip was cut; there was a little trickle of blood down the corner of her mouth. Her tongue came out, tasted, and then licked it away.

KATHERINE ANNE PORTER

Virgin Violeta

Violeta, nearly fifteen years old, sat on a hassock, hugging her knees and watching Carlos, her cousin, and her sister Blanca, who were reading poetry aloud by turns at the long table.

Occasionally she glanced down at her own feet, clad in thick-soled brown sandals, the toes turned in a trifle. Their ugliness distressed her, and she pulled her short skirt over them until the beltline sagged under her loose, dark blue woolen blouse. Then she straightened up, with a full, silent breath, uncovering the sandals again. Each time her eyes moved under shy lids to Carlos, to see if he had noticed;

he never did notice. Disappointed, a little troubled, Violeta would sit very still for a while, listening and watching.

> " *'This torment of love which is in my heart:*
> *I know that I suffer it, but I do not know why.'* "

Blanca's voice was thin, with a whisper in it. She seemed anxious to keep the poetry all for Carlos and herself. Her shawl, embroidered in yellow on gray silk, slipped from her shoulders whenever she inclined toward the lamp. Carlos would lift the tassel of fringe nearest him between finger and thumb and toss it deftly into place. Blanca's nod, her smile, were the perfection of amiable indifference. But her voice wavered, caught on the word. She had always to begin again the line she was reading.

Carlos would slant his pale eyes at Blanca; then he would resume his pose, gaze fixed on a small painting on the white paneled wall over Violeta's head. "Pious Interview between the Most Holy Virgin Queen of Heaven and Her Faithful Servant St. Ignatius Loyola," read the thin metal plate on the carved and gilded frame. The Virgin, with enameled face set in a detached simper, forehead bald of eyebrows, extended one hand remotely over the tonsured head of the saint, who groveled in a wooden posture of ecstasy. Very ugly and old-fashioned, thought Violeta, but a perfectly proper picture; there was nothing to stare at. But Carlos kept squinting his eyelids at it mysteriously, and never moved his eyes from it save to glance at Blanca. His furry, golden eyebrows were knotted sternly, resembling a tangle of crochet wool. He never seemed to be interested except when it was his turn to read. He read in a thrilling voice. Violeta thought his mouth and chin were very beautiful. A tiny spot of light on his slightly moistened underlip disturbed her, she did not know why.

Blanca stopped reading, bowed her head and sighed lightly, her mouth half open. It was one of her habits. As the sound of voices had lulled Mamacita to sleep beside her sewing basket, now the silence roused her. She looked about her with a vivacious smile on her whole face, except her eyes, which were drowsed and weary.

"Go on with your reading, dear children. I heard every word. Violeta, don't fidget, please, sweet little daughter. Carlos, what is the hour?"

Mamacita liked being chaperon to Blanca. Violeta wondered why Mamacita considered Blanca so very attractive, but she did. She was always saying to Papacito, "Blanquita blooms like a lily!" And Papacito would say, "It is better if she conducts herself like one!" And Mamacita said once to Carlos, "Even if you are my nephew, still you must go home at a reasonable hour!"

"The hour is early, Doña Paz." St. Anthony himself could not have exceeded in respect the pose of Carlos' head toward his aunt. She smiled and relapsed into a shallow nap, as a cat rises from the rug, turns and lies down again.

Violeta did not move, or answer Mamacita. She had the silence and watchfulness of a young wild animal, but no native wisdom. She was at home from the convent in Tacubaya for the first time in almost a year. There they taught her modesty, chastity, silence, obedience, with a little French and music and some arithmetic. She did as she was told, but it was all very confusing, because she could not understand why the things that happen outside of people were so different from what she felt inside of her. Everybody went about doing the same things every day, precisely as if there were nothing else going to happen, ever; and all the time she was certain there was something simply tremendously exciting waiting for her outside the convent. Life was going to unroll itself like a long, gay carpet for her to walk upon. She saw herself wearing a long veil, and it would trail and flutter over this carpet as she came out of church. There would be six flower girls and two pages, the way there had been at Cousin Sancha's wedding.

Of course she didn't mean a wedding. Silly! Cousin Sancha had been quite old, almost twenty-four, and Violeta meant for life to begin at once—next year, anyway. It would be more like a festival. She wanted to wear red poppies in her hair and dance. Life would always be very gay, with no one about telling you that almost everything you said and did was wrong. She would be free to read poetry, too, and stories about love, without having to hide them in her copybooks. Even Carlos did not know that she had learned nearly all his poems by heart. She had for a year been cutting them from magazines, keeping them in the pages of her books, in order to read them during study hours.

Several shorter ones were concealed in her missal, and the thrilling music of strange words drowned the chorus of bell and choir. There was one about the ghosts of nuns returning to the old square before their ruined convent, dancing in the moonlight with the shades of lovers forbidden them in life, treading with bared feet on broken glass as a penance for their loves. Violeta would shake all over when she read this, and lift swimming eyes to the delicate spears of candlelight on the altar.

She was certain she would be like those nuns someday. She would dance for joy over shards of broken glass. But where begin? She had sat here in this room, on this very hassock, comfortingly near Mamacita, through the summer evenings of vacation, ever since she could remember. Sometimes it was a happiness to be assured that nothing was expected of her but to follow Mamacita about and be a good girl. It gave her time to dream about life—that is, the future. For of course everything beautiful and unexpected would happen later on, when she grew as tall as Blanca and was allowed to come home from the convent for good and all. She would then be miraculously lovely—Blanca would look perfectly dull beside her—and she would dance with fascinating young men like those who rode by on Sunday mornings, making their horses prance in the bright, shallow street on their way to the *paseo* in Chapultepec Park. She would appear on the balcony above, wearing a blue dress, and everyone would ask who that enchanting girl could be. And Carlos, Carlos! He would understand at last that she had read and loved his poems always.

> *"The nuns are dancing with bare feet*
> *On broken glass in the cobbled street."*

That one above all the rest. She felt it had been written for her. She was even one of the nuns, the youngest and best-loved one, ghostly silent, dancing forever and ever under the moonlight to the shivering tune of old violins.

Mamacita moved her knee uneasily, so that Violeta's head

slipped from it, and she almost lost her balance. She sat up, prickling all over with shyness for fear the others would know why she had hidden her face on Mamacita's lap. But no one saw. Mamacita was always lecturing her about things. At such moments it was hard to believe that Blanca was not the favorite child. "You must not run through the house so." "You must brush your hair more smoothly." "And what is this I hear about your using your sister's face powder?"

Blanca, listening, would eye her with superior calm and say nothing. It was really very hard, knowing that Blanca was nicer only because she was allowed to powder and perfume herself and still gave herself such airs about it. Carlos, who used to bring her sugared limes and long strips of dried *membrillo* from the markets, calling her his dear, amusing, modest Violeta, now simply did not know she was present. There were times when Violeta wished to cry, passionately, so everyone could hear her. But what about? And how explain to Mamacita? She would say, "What have you to cry for? And besides, consider the feelings of others in this house and control your moods."

Papacito would say, "What you need is a good renovating." That was his word for a spanking. He would say sternly to Mamacita, "I think her moral nature needs repairment." He and Mamacita seemed to have some mysterious understanding about things. Mamacita's eyes were always perfectly clear when she looked at Papacito, and she would answer: "You are right. I will look after this." Then she would be very severe with Violeta. Papacito always said to the girls: "It is your fault without exception when Mamacita is annoyed with you. So be careful."

But Mamacita never stayed annoyed for long, and afterward it was beautiful to curl up near her, snuggling into her shoulder, and smell the nice, crinkled, perfumed hair at the nape of her neck. But when she was angry her eyes had a considering expression, as if one were a stranger, and she would say, "You are the greatest of my problems." Violeta had often been a problem and it was very humiliating.

¡Ay de mi! Violeta gave a sharp sigh and sat up straight. She wanted to stretch her arms up and yawn, not because she was sleepy but because something inside her felt as if it were enclosed in a cage too small for it, and she could not breathe. Like those poor parrots in the markets, stuffed into tiny wicker cages so that they bulged through the withes, gasping and panting, waiting for someone to come and rescue them.

Church was a terrible, huge cage, but it seemed too small. "Oh, my, I always laugh, to keep from crying!" A silly verse Carlos used to say. Through her eyelashes his face looked suddenly pale and soft, as if he might have tears on his cheeks. Oh, Carlos! But of course he would never cry for anything. She was frightened to find that her own eyes were steeped in tears; they were going to run down her face; she couldn't stop them. Her head bowed over and her chin seemed to be curling up. Where on earth was her handkerchief? A huge, clean, white linen one, almost like a boy's handkerchief. How horrid! The folded corner scratched her eyelids. Sometimes she cried in church when the music wailed terribly and the girls sat in veiled rows, all silent except for the clinking of their beads slipping through their fingers. They were all strangers to her then; what if they knew her thoughts? Suppose she should say aloud, "I love Carlos!" The idea made her blush all over, until her forehead perspired and her hands turned red. She would begin praying frantically, "Oh, Mary! Oh, Mary! Queen Mother of mercy!" while deep underneath her words her thoughts were rushing aloud in a kind of trance: Oh, dear God, that's my secret; that's a secret between You and me. I should die if anybody knew!

She turned her eyes again to the pair at the long table just in time to see once more the shawl beginning to slip, ever so little, from Blanca's shoulder. A tight shudder of drawn threads played along Violeta's skin, and grew quite intolerable when Carlos reached out to take the fringe in his long fingers. His wrist turned with a delicate toss, the shawl settled into place, Blanca smiled and stammered and bit her lip.

Violeta could not bear to see it. No, no. She wanted to hold her hands over her heart tightly, to quell the slow, burning ache. It felt like a little jar filled with flames, which she could not smother down. It was cruel of Blanca and Carlos to sit there and read and be so pleased with each other without once thinking of her! Yet what could she say if they noticed her? They never did notice.

Blanca rose.

"I am tired of the old poetry. It is all too sad. What else whall we read?"

"Let's have a great deal of gay, modern poetry," suggested Carlos, whose own verses were considered extremely gay and modern. Violeta was always shocked when he called them amusing. He couldn't mean it. It was only his way of pretending he wasn't sad when he wrote them.

"Read me all your new ones again." Blanca was always appreciating Carlos. You could hear it in her voice underneath, like a little trickle of sugar. And Carlos let her do it. He seemed always to be condescending to Blanca a little. But Blanca could never see it, because she really didn't think of anything but the way she had her hair fixed or whether people thought she was pretty. Violeta longed to make a naughty face at Blanca, who posed ridiculously, leaning over the table.

Above the red silk lamp shade her face was not sallow as usual. The thin nose and small lips cast shadows on her cheek. She hated being pale, and had the habit, while reading, of smoothing her cheeks round and round with two fingers, first one cheek and then the other, until deep red spots would burn in them for a long while. Violeta wished to shriek after watching Blanca do this for hours at a time. Why did not Mamacita speak to her about it? It was the worst sort of fidgeting.

"I haven't the new ones with me," said Carlos.

"Then let it be the old ones," agreed Blanca gaily.

She moved to the bookshelves, Carlos beside her. They could not find his book. Their hands touched as fingers sought titles. Something in the intimate murmur of their voices wounded Violeta acutely. Sharing some delightful secret, they were purposely shutting her out. She spoke.

"If you want your book, Carlos, I can find it." At the sound of her own voice she felt calm and firm and equal to anything. By her tone she tried to shut Blanca out.

They turned and regarded her without interest.

"And where may it be, infant?" Carlos' voice always had that chilling edge on it when he was not reading aloud, and his eyes explored. With a glance he seemed to see all one's faults. Violeta remembered her feet and drew down her skirts. The sight of Blanca's narrow, gray satin slippers was hateful.

"I have it. I have had it for a whole week." She eyed the tip of Blanca's nose, hoping they would understand she wished to say, "You see, I have treasured it!"

She got up, feeling a little clumsy, and walked away with a curious imitation of Blanca's grown-up gait. It made her dreadfully aware of her long, straight legs in their ribbed stockings.

"I will help you search," called Carlos, as if he had thought of something interesting, and he followed. Over his suddenly near shoulder she saw Blanca's face. It looked very vague and faraway, like a distressed doll's. Carlos' eyes were enormous, and he smiled steadily. She wished to run away. He said something in a low voice. She could not understand him at all, and it was impossible to find the lamp cord in the narrow, dark hallway. She was frightened at the soft *pad-pad* of his rubber heels so close behind her as they went without speaking through the chill dining room, full of the odor of fruit that has been all day in a closed place. When they entered the small, open sunroom over the entrance of the patio, the moonlight seemed almost warm, it was so radiant after the shadows of the house. Violeta turned over a huddle of books on the small table, but she did not see them clearly; and her hand shook so, she could not take hold of anything.

Carlos' hand came up in a curve, settled upon hers and held fast. His roundish, smooth cheek and blond eyebrows hovered, swooped. His mouth touched hers and made a tiny smacking sound. She felt herself wrench and twist away as if a hand pushed her violently. And in that second his hand was over her mouth, soft and warm, and his eyes were staring at her, fearfully close. Violeta opened her eyes wide also and peered up at him. She expected to sink into a look warm and gentle, like the touch of his palm. Instead, she felt suddenly, sharply hurt, as if she had collided with a chair in the dark. His eyes were bright and shallow, almost like the eyes of Pepe, the macaw. His pale, fluffy eyebrows were arched; his mouth smiled tightly. A sick thumping began in the pit of her stomach, as it always did when she was called up to explain things to Mother Superior. Something was terribly wrong. Her heart pounded until she seemed about to smother. She was angry with all her might, and turned her head aside in a hard jerk.

"Keep your hand off my mouth!"

"Then be quiet, you silly child!" The words were astounding, but the way he said them was more astounding still, as if they were allies in some shameful secret. Her teeth rattled with chill.

"I will tell my mother! Shame on you for kissing me!"

"I did not kiss you except a little brotherly kiss, Violeta, precisely as I kiss Blanca. Don't be absurd!"

"You do not kiss Blanca. I heard her tell my mother she has never been kissed by a man!"

"But I do kiss her—as a cousin, nothing more. It does not count. We are relatives just the same. What did you think?"

Oh, she had made a hideous mistake. She knew she was blushing until her forehead throbbed. Her breath was gone, but she must explain. "I thought—a kiss—meant—meant—" She could not finish.

"Ah, you're so young, like a little newborn calf," said Carlos. His voice trembled in a strange way. "You smell like a nice baby, freshly washed with white soap! Imagine such a baby being angry at a kiss from her cousin! Shame on you, Violeta!"

He was loathsome. She saw herself before him, almost as if his face were a mirror. Her mouth was too large; her face was simply a moon; her hair was ugly in the tight convent braids.

"Oh, I'm so sorry!" she whispered.

"For what?" His voice had the cutting edge again. "Come, where is the book?"

"I don't know," she said, trying not to cry.

"Well, then, let us go back, or Mamacita will scold you."

"Oh, no, no. I can't go in there. Blanca will see—Mamacita will ask questions. I want to stay here. I want to run away—to kill myself!"

"Nonsense!" said Carlos. "Come with me this minute. What did you expect when you came out here alone with me?"

He turned and started away. She was shamefully, incredibly in the wrong. She had behaved like an immodest girl. It was all bitterly real and unbelievable, like a nightmare that went on and on and no one heard you calling to be waked up. She followed, trying to hold up her head.

Mamacita nodded, shining, crinkled hair stiffly arranged, chin on white collar. Blanca sat like a stone in her deep chair, holding a small gray-and-gold book in her lap. Her angry eyes threw out a look that coiled back upon itself like a whiplash, and the pupils became suddenly blank and bright as Carlos' had.

Violeta folded down on her hassock and gathered up her knees. She stared at the carpet to hide her reddened eyes, for it terrified her to see the way eyes could give away such cruel stories about people.

"I found the book here, where it belonged," said Blanca. "I am tired now. It is very late. We shall not read."

Violeta wished to cry in real earnest now. It was the last blow that Blanca should have found the book. A kiss meant nothing at all, and Carlos had walked away as if he had forgotten her. It was all mixed up with the white rivers of moonlight and the smell of warm fruit and a cold dampness on her lips that made a tiny, smacking sound. She trembled and leaned over until her forehead touched Mamacita's lap. She could not look up, ever, ever again.

The low voices sounded contentious; thin metal wires twanged in the air around them.

"But I do not care to read any more, I tell you."

"Very well, I shall go at once. But I am leaving for Paris on Wednesday, and shall not see you again until the fall."

"It would be like you to go without even stopping in to say good-by."

Even when they were angry they still talked to each other like two grown-up people wrapped together in a secret. The sound of his soft, padding rubber heels came near.

"Good night, my dearest Doña Paz. I have had an enchanting evening."

Mamacita's knees moved; she meant to rise.

"What—asleep, Violeta? Well, let us hear often from you, my dear nephew. Your little cousins and I will miss you greatly."

Mamacita was wide-awake and smiling, holding Carlos' hands. They kissed. Carlos turned to Blanca and bent to kiss her. She swept him into the folds of the gray shawl, but turned her cheek for his salute. Violeta rose, her knees trembling. She turned her head from side to side to close out the sight of the macaw eyes coming closer and closer, the tight, smiling mouth ready to swoop. When he touched her, she wavered for a moment, then slid up and back against the wall. She heard herself screaming uncontrollably.

Mamacita sat upon the side of the bed and patted Violeta's cheek. Her curved hand was warm and gentle and so were her eyes. Violeta choked a little and turned her face away.

"I have explained to Papacito that you quarreled with your cousin Carlos and were very rude to him. Papacito says you need a good renovating." Mamacita's voice was soft and reassuring. Violeta lay without a pillow, the ruffled collar of her nightgown standing up about her chin. She did not answer. Even to whisper hurt her.

"We are going to the country this week and you shall live in the garden all summer. Then you won't be so nervous. You are quite a young lady now, and you must learn to control your nerves."

"Yes, Mamacita." The look on Mamacita's face was very hard to bear. She seemed to be asking questions about very hidden thoughts—those thoughts that were not true at all and could never be talked about with anyone. Everything she could remember in her whole life seemed to have melted together in a confusion and misery that could not be explained because it was all changed and uncertain.

She wanted to sit up, take Mamacita around the neck and say, "Something dreadful happened to me—I don't know what," but her heart closed up hard and aching, and she sighed with all her breath. Even Mamacita's breast had become a cold, strange place. Her blood ran back and forth in her, crying terribly, but when the sound came up to her lips it was only a small whimper, like a puppy's.

"You must not cry any more," said Mamacita after a long pause. Then: "Good night, my poor child. This impression will pass." Mamacita's kiss felt cold on Violeta's cheek.

Whether the impression passed or not, no word of it was spoken again. Violeta and the family spent the summer in the country. She refused to read Carlos' poetry, though Mamacita encouraged her to do so. She would not even listen to his letters from Paris. She quarreled on more equal terms with her sister Blanca, feeling that there was no longer so great a difference of experience to separate them. A painful unhappiness possessed her at times, because she could not settle the questions brooding in her mind. Sometimes she amused herself making ugly caricatures of Carlos.

In the early autumn she returned to school, weeping and complaining to her mother that she hated the convent. There was, she declared as she watched her boxes being tied up, nothing to be learned there.

R. PRAWER JHABVALA

My First Marriage

Last week Rahul went on a hunger-strike. He didn't have to suffer long—his family got very frightened (he is the only son) and by the second day they were ready to do anything he wanted, even to let him marry me. So he had a big meal, and then he came to tell me of his achievement. He was so proud and happy that I too pretended to be happy. Now his father and Daddy are friends again, and they sit downstairs in the study and talk together about their university days in England. His mother too comes to the house, and yesterday his married sister Kamla paid me a visit. The last time I had met Kamla was when she told me all those things on their veranda, but neither of us seemed to have any recollection of that. Instead we had a very nice conversation about her husband's promotion and the annual flower show for which she had been asked to organize a raffle. Mama walks around the house looking pleased with herself and humming snatches of the national anthem (out of tune—she is completely unmusical). No one ever mentions M. any more.

It is two years now since he went away. I don't know where he is or what he is doing. Perhaps he is meditating somewhere in the Himalayas, or wandering by the banks of the Ganges with an orange robe and a begging-bowl; or perhaps he is just living in another town, trying to start a newspaper or a school. Sometimes I ask myself: can there really have been such a man? But it is not a question to which I require any answer.

The first time I saw M., I was just going out to tennis with Rahul. I hardly glanced at him—he was just one of the people who came to see Daddy. But he returned many times, and I heard Daddy say: "That young man is a nuisance." "Of course," said Mama in a sarcastic way, "you can never say no to anyone." Daddy looked shy: it was true, he found it difficult to refuse people. He is the Director of Education, and because it is an important position, people are always coming, both to the house and to his office, to ask him to do something for them. Mostly there is nothing he can do, but because he is so nice and polite to them, they keep coming again. Then often Mama steps in.

One day, just as I was going out to Rahul's house, I heard her shouting outside the door of the study. "The Director is a busy man!" she was shouting. She had her back against the door and held her arms stretched out;

M. stood in front of her, and his head was lowered. "Day after day you come and eat his life up!" she said.

I feel very embarrassed when I hear Mama shouting at people, so I went away quickly. But when I was walking down the road, he suddenly came behind me. He said, "Why are you walking so fast?"

I said nothing. I thought it was very rude of him to speak to me at all.

"You are running away," he said.

Then in spite of myself I had to laugh: "From what?"

"From the Real," he said, and he spoke so seriously that I was impressed and stood still in the middle of the road and looked at him.

He was not really young—not young like I am, or like Rahul. His hair was already going grey and he had lines round his eyes. But what eyes they were, how full of wisdom and experience! And he was looking at me with them. I can't describe how I felt suddenly.

He said he wanted Daddy to open a new department in the university. A department for moral training. He explained the scheme to me and we both stood still in the road. His eyes glowed. I understood at once; of course, not everything—I am not a brilliant person such as he—but I understood it was important and even grand. Here were many new ideas, which made life seem quite different. I began to see that I had been living wrongly because I had been brought up to think wrongly. Everything I thought important, and Daddy and Mama and Rahul and everyone, was not important: these were the frivolities of life we were caught up in. For the first time someone was explaining to me the nature of reality. I promised to help him and to speak to Daddy. I was excited and couldn't stop thinking of everything he had said and the way he had said it.

He often telephoned. I waited for his calls and was impatient and restless till they came. But I was also a little ashamed to talk to him because I could not tell him that I had succeeded. I spoke to Daddy many times. I said, "Education is no use without a firm moral basis."

"How philosophical my little girl is getting," Daddy said and smiled and was pleased that I was taking an interest in higher things.

Mama said, "Don't talk so much; it's not nice in a young girl."

When M. telephoned I could only say, "I'm trying."

"You are not trying!" he said; he spoke sternly to me. "You are thinking of your own pleasures only, of your tennis and games."

He was right—I often played tennis, and now that my examinations were finished, I spent a lot of time at the Club and went to the cinema and read novels. When he spoke to me, I realized all that was wrong; so that every time he telephoned I was thoughtful for many hours afterwards and when Rahul came to fetch me for tennis, I said I had a headache.

But I tried to explain to Rahul. He listened carefully; Rahul listens carefully to everything I say. He becomes very serious, and his eyes, which are already very large, become even larger. He looks so sweet then, just as he did when he was a little boy. I remember Rahul as a little boy, for we always played together. His father and Daddy were great friends, almost like brothers. So Rahul and I grew up together, and later it was decided we would be married. Everyone was happy: I also, and Rahul. We were to be married quite soon, for we had both finished our college and Rahul's father had already got him a good job in a business firm, with very fine prospects.

"You see, Rahul, we live in nice houses and have nice clothes and good education and everything, and all the time we don't know what reality is."

Rahul frowned a bit, the way he used to do over his sums when they were difficult; but he nodded and looked at me with his big sweet eyes and was ready to listen to everything else I would tell him. Rahul has very smooth cheeks and they are a little bit pink because he is so healthy.

One day when M. telephoned he asked me to go and meet him. At first I tried to say no, but I knew I really wanted to go. He called me to a coffee-house I had never been to before, and I felt shy when going in—there were many men and no girls at all. Everyone looked at me; some of them may have been students from the university and perhaps they knew me. It was noisy in there and full of smoke and smell of fritters and chutney. The tablecloths were dirty and so were the bearers' uniforms. But he was there, waiting for me. I had often tried to recall his face but I never could; now I saw it and—of course, of course, I cried to myself, that was how it was, how could I forget.

Then I began to meet him every day. Sometimes we met in that coffee-house, at other times in a little park where there was a broken swing and an old tomb and clerks came to eat their lunch out of tiffin-carriers. It was the end of winter and the sky was pale blue with little white lines on it and the sun was just beginning to get hot again and there were scarlet creepers all over the tomb and green parrots flew about. When I went home, I would lie on the bed in my room and think. Rahul came and I said I had a headache. I hardly knew anything anyone was saying. I ate very little. Mama often came into my room and asked, "Where did you go today?" She was very sweet and gentle, the way she always is when she wants to find out something from you. I would tell her anything that came into my head —an old college friend had come from Poona, we had been to the cinema together—"Which cinema?" Mama said, still sweet and gentle and tidying the handkerchiefs in my drawer. I would even tell her the story of the film I had not seen. "Tomorrow I'm meeting her again." "No, tomorrow I want you to come with me to Meena auntie—"

It began to be difficult to get out of the house. Mama watched me every minute, and when she saw me ready to leave, she stood in the doorway: "Today you are coming with me."

"I told you, I have to meet—"

"You are coming with me!"

We were both angry and shouted. Daddy came out of the study. He told Mama, "She is not a child. . . ."

Then Mama started to shout at him and I ran out of the house and did not look back, though I could hear her calling me.

When I told M., he said, "You had better come with me." I also saw there was no other way. On Friday afternoons Mama goes to a committee meeting of the All-India Ladies' Council, so that was the best time. I bundled up all my clothes and jewels in a sheet and I walked out of the house. Faqir Chand, our butler, saw me, but he said nothing—

probably he thought I was sending my clothes to the washerman. M. was waiting for me in a tonga by the post office and he helped me climb up and sit beside him; the tonga was a very old and shaky one, and the driver was also old and so was the horse. We went very slowly, first by the river, past the Fort and through all the bazaars, he and I sitting side by side at the back of the tonga with my bundle between us.

We had such a strange wedding. I laugh even now when I think of it. He had a friend who was a sign-painter and had a workshop on the other side of the river. The workshop was really only a shed, but they made it very nice—they turned all the signboards to the wall and they hung my saris over them and over the saris they hung flower garlands. It looked really artistic. They also bought sweetmeats and nuts and put them on a long table which they had borrowed from a carpenter. Several friends of his came and quite a lot of people who lived in sheds and huts near by. There was a priest and a fire was lit and we sat in front of it and the priest chanted the holy verses. I was feeling very hot because of the fire and of course my face was completely covered by the sari. It wasn't a proper wedding sari, but my own old red sari which I had last worn when Mama gave a tea-party for the professors' wives in our drawing-room, with cakes from Wenger's.

M. got very impatient, he kept telling the priest, "Now hurry hurry, we have heard all that before."

The priest was offended and said, "These are all holy words."

I couldn't help laughing under my sari, even though I

was crying at the same time because I was thinking of Daddy and Rahul and Mama.

There was a quarrel—his friends also told him to keep quiet and let the priest say his verses in the proper manner, and he got angry and shouted, "Is it my marriage or yours?"

At last it was finished and we were married and everyone ate sweetmeats and nuts, even people who just wandered in from the road and whom no one knew.

We stayed a few days with his friend. There was a little room built out of planks just off the workshop and in that we all slept at night, rolled up in blankets. In the day, when the friend painted signs, we stayed in the room by ourselves, M. and I, and no one came in to disturb us. When he slept, I would look at him and look; I studied all the lines on his face. After I had looked my fill, I would shut my eyes and try and see his face in my mind, and when I opened them again, there he was really, his real face, and I cried out loud with joy.

After some days we went on a bus to Niripat. The journey was four hours long and the bus was crowded with farmers and labourers and many old women carrying little bundles. There was a strong smell of poor people who can't afford to change their clothes very often and of the food which the old women ate out of their bundles and the petrol from the bus. I began to feel a little sick. I often get car-sick: when we used to drive up to Naini Tal for the summer holidays, Daddy always had to stop the car several times so that I could go out and take fresh air; and Mama would give me lemon-drops to suck and rub my temples with eau-de-cologne.

In Niripat we stayed with M.'s cousin, who had a little

brick house just outside the town. They were a big family, and the women lived in one side of the house, in a little set of dark rooms with only metal trunks and beds in them, and the men on the other side. But I ran all over the house; I was singing and laughing all the time. In the evenings I sat with the men and listened to them talking about religion and philosophy and their business (they had a grinding mill); and during the day I helped the women with their household work. M. and I went out for walks and sometimes we went swimming in a pond. The women of the house teased me a lot because I liked M. so much. "But look at him," they said, "he is so dark; and see! his hair is going grey like an old man's." Or, "He is just a loafer—it is only talking with him and never any work." I pretended to be annoyed with them (of course, I knew they were only joking) and that made them laugh more than ever. One of them said, "Now it is very fine, but just wait, in the end her state will be the same as Savitri's."

"Savitri?" I said.

So that was how I first heard about Savitri and the children. At first I was unhappy, but M. explained everything. He had been married very young and to a simple girl from a village. After some years he left her. She understood it was necessary for him to leave her because he had a task to fulfil in the world in which she could not help him. She went back to her parents, with the children. She was happy now, because she saw it was her duty to stay at home and look after the children and lead the good, simple, self-sacrificing life of a mother. He talked of her with affection: she was patient and good. I too learned to love her. I thought of her in the village, with the children, quietly doing her household tasks; early in the mornings and in the evenings she said her prayers. So her life passed. He had gone to see her a few times and she had welcomed him and been glad; but when he went away again, she never tried to keep him. I thought how it would be if he went away from me, but I could not even bear the idea. My heart hurt terribly and I stifled a cry. From that I saw how much nobler and more advanced Savitri was than I; and I hoped that, if the time ever came, I too could be strong like her. But not yet. Not yet. We sold my pearl brooch and sent money to her; he always sent money to her when he had it. Once he said of her: "She is a candle burning in a window of the world," and that was how I always thought of her— as a candle burning for him with a humble flame.

I had not yet written to Daddy and Mama, but I wrote to Rahul. I wrote, "Everything is for the best, Rahul. I often think about you. Please tell everyone that I am all right and happy." M. and I went to the post office together to buy a stamp and post the letter. On the way back he said, "You must write to your father also. He must listen to our ideas." How proud I was when he said *our* ideas.

Daddy and Mama came to Niripat. Daddy sent me a letter in which it said they were waiting for me at the Victoria Hotel. M. took me there, and then went away; he said I must talk to them and explain everything. The Victoria Hotel is the only hotel in Niripat and it is not very grand— it is certainly not the sort of hotel in which Mama is used to staying. In front there is the Victoria Restaurant where meals can be had at a reduced rate on a monthly basis; there is an open passage at the side which leads to the hotel rooms. Some of the guests had pulled their beds out into the passage and were sitting on them: I noticed a very fat man in a dhoti and an undervest saying his prayers. But Daddy and Mama were inside their room.

It was a very small room with two big beds in it and a table with a blue cotton tablecloth in the middle. Mama was lying on one of the beds; she was crying, and when I came in, she cried more. Daddy and I embraced each other, but Mama turned her face away and pressed her eyes with her handkerchief and the tears rolled right down into her blouse. It made me impatient to see her like that: every mother must part with her daughter some time, so what was there to cry about? I squeezed Daddy's hands, to show him how happy I was, but then he too turned his face away from me and he coughed. Here we were meeting after so many days, and they were both behaving in a ridiculous manner. I spoke to them quite sharply: "Every individual being must choose his own life and I have chosen mine."

"Don't, darling," Daddy said as if something were hurting him.

Mama suddenly shouted, "You are my shame and disgrace!"

"Quietly, quietly," Daddy said.

I felt like shouting back at her, but I controlled myself; I had not come there to quarrel with her, even if she had come to quarrel with me. I was a wiser person now than I had been. So I only said: "There are aspects of life which you will never grasp."

A little servant-boy came in with tea on a tray. Mama sat up on the bed—she is always very keen on her tea—but after a while she sank back again and said in a fainting sort of voice, "There is something dirty in the milk." I had a look and there were only bits of straw, from the cowshed, which I fished out easily with a tea-spoon.

Daddy gave a big sigh and said, "You had better let me speak with the young man."

So then I was happy again: I knew that when Daddy really spoke to him and got to know him, he would soon realize what sort of a person M. was and everything would be all right.

And everything was all right. It was true, Daddy couldn't start the department of moral training for him, as we had hoped, because the university didn't have enough funds for a new department; and also, Daddy said, he couldn't get him an academic post because M. didn't have the necessary qualifications. (How stupid are these rules and regulations! Here was a wonderful gifted person like M., with great ideas and wide experience of life, who had so much to pass on; yet he had to take a backward place to some poor little M.A. or Ph.D. who knows nothing of life at all except what he has read in other people's books.) So all Daddy could do was get him a post as secretary to one of the college principals; and I think it was very nice of M. to accept it, because it was not the sort of post a person such as he had a right to expect. But he was always like that: he knew nothing of petty pride and never stood on his dignity, unlike many other people who have really no dignity at all to stand on.

I was sorry to leave Niripat where I had been so happy with everyone and to go home again. But of course it was different now, because M. was with me. We had the big guest-room at the back of the house and at night we made our beds out on the lawn. Sometimes I thought how funny it was—only a few weeks ago Mama had tried to turn him out of the house and here he was back in the best guest-room. It is true that the wheel of fate has many unexpected revolutions. I think he quite liked living in the house, though I was afraid at first he would feel stifled with so many servants and all that furniture and carpets and clocks and Mama's china dinner-services. But he was too great in soul to be bothered by these trivial things; he transcended them and led his life and thought his thoughts in the same way as he would have done if he had been living in some little hut in the jungle.

If only Mama had had a different character. But she is too sunk in her own social station and habits to be able to look out and appreciate anything higher. She thinks if a person has not been abroad and doesn't wear suits and open doors for ladies, he is an inferior type of person. If M. had tried, I know he could have used a knife and fork quite as well as Mama or anyone, but why should he have tried? And there were other things like not making a noise when you drink your tea, which are just trivial little conventions we should all rise above. I often tried to explain this to Mama but I could never make her understand. So it became often quite embarrassing at meal-times, with Mama looking at M. and pretending she couldn't eat her own food on account of the way he was eating his. M. of course never noticed, and I felt so ashamed of Mama that in the end I also refused to use any cutlery and ate with my hands. Daddy never said anything—in fact, Daddy said very little at all nowadays, and spent long hours in his office and went to a lot of meetings and, when he came home, he only sat in his study and did not come out to talk to us.

I often thought about Rahul. He had never answered my letter and when I tried to telephone, they said he was not at home. But I wanted very much to see him; there were so many things I had to tell him about. So one day I went to his house. The servants made me wait on the veranda and then Rahul's married sister Kamla came out. Kamla is a very ambitious person and she is always scheming for her husband's promotion (he is in the Ministry of Defence) so that she can take precedence over the other wives in his department. I was not surprised at the way she talked to me. I know a person like Kamla will always think only petty thoughts and doesn't understand that there is anything transcending the everyday life in which she is sunk up to her ears. So I let her say what she wanted and when she told me to go away, I went. When Mama found out that I had been to Rahul's house, she was furious. "All right, so you have lost all pride for yourself, but for your family—at least think of us!" At the word pride I laughed out loud: Mama's ideas of pride were so different from mine and M.'s. But I was sorry that they wouldn't let me see Rahul.

M. went out every day, and I thought he went to his job in the university. But one day Daddy called me into his study and he said that M. had lost his job because he hadn't been going there for weeks. I had a little shock at first, but then I thought it is all right, whatever he wants to do is all right; and anyway, it hadn't been a suitable post for him in the first place. I told Daddy so.

Daddy played with his silver paper-knife and he didn't

look at me at all; then he said, "You know he has been married before?" and still he didn't look at me.

I don't know how Daddy found out—I suppose he must have been making inquiries, it is the sort of thing people in our station of life always do about other people, we are so mistrustful—but I answered him quite calmly. I tried to explain to him about Savitri.

After a while Daddy said, "I only wanted you to know that your marriage is not legal and can be dissolved any time you want."

Then I told him that marriages are not made in the sight of the law but in the sight of God, and that in the sight of God both Savitri and I were married to M., she there and I here. Daddy turned his head away and looked out of the window.

M. told me that he wanted to start a school and that he could do so if Daddy got him a grant from the Ministry. I thought it was a very exciting idea and we talked a lot about it that night, as we lay together on our beds. He had many wonderful ideas about how a school should be run and said that the children should be taught to follow only their instincts which would lead them to the highest Good. He talked so beautifully, like a prophet, a saint. I could hardly sleep all night, and first thing in the morning I talked to Daddy. Unfortunately Mama was listening at the door—she has a bad habit of doing that—and suddenly she came bursting in. "Why don't you leave your father alone?" she cried. "Isn't it enough that we give you both food and shelter?"

I said, "Mama please, I'm talking important business with Daddy."

She began to say all sorts of things about M. and why he had married me. Daddy tried to keep her quiet but she was beyond herself by that time, so I just covered my ears with my hands and ran out. She came after me, still shouting these horrible things.

There in the hall was M., and when I tried to run past him, he stopped me and took my hands from my ears and made me listen to everything Mama was saying. She got more and more furious, and then she went into one of her hysterical fits, in which she throws herself down and beats her head on the floor and tears at her clothes. Daddy tried to lift her up, but of course she is too heavy for him. She went on screaming and shouting at M.

M. said, "Go and get your things," so I went and wrapped everything up in the sheet again, his things and mine, and he slung the bundle over his shoulder and went out of the house, with me walking behind him.

I hoped we would go back to Niripat, but he wanted to stay in the city because he had several schemes in mind—there was the school, and he also had hopes of starting a newspaper in which he could print all his ideas. So he had to go round and see a lot of people, in Ministries and so on. Sometimes he got quite discouraged because it was so difficult to make people understand. Then he looked tired and the lines on his face became very deep and I felt such love and pity for him. But he had great inner strength, and next day he always started on his rounds again, as fresh and hopeful as before.

We had no proper home at that time, but lived in several places. There was the sign-painter, and another friend had a bookshop in one of the government markets with a little room at the back where we could stay with him; and once we found a model house which was left over from a low-cost housing exhibition and we lived in that till workmen came to tear it down. There were plenty of places where we could stay for a few days or even weeks. In the evenings there were always many friends and all sat and discussed their ideas, and some of them recited poetry or played the flute, so that sometimes we didn't go to sleep at all. We never had any worries about money—M. said if one doesn't think about money, one doesn't need it, and how true that is. Daddy sent me a cheque every month, care of the friend who kept the bookshop, and we still had some of my jewellery which we could sell whenever we wanted; so there was even money to send to Savitri and the children.

Once I met Rahul, quite by chance. That was at the time when we had just moved out of the exhibition house. M. had to go to one of the Ministries to see an Under-Secretary, and I was taking our bundle to an orphanage, run by a friend of M.'s, where we were going to stay. I was waiting for a bus, holding the bundle; it wasn't heavy at all any more, so there was no need to take a tonga. Rahul came out of a music-shop with some records which he had just bought (he is very fond of dance-records—how often we have danced together to his gramophone!). I called to him and when he didn't hear me, I went up to him. He lowered his eyes and wouldn't look at me and hardly greeted me.

"Rahul," I said in the stern voice I always use with him when I think he is misbehaving.

"Why did you do it?" he said. "My family are very angry

with you and I'm also angry." He sulked, but he looked so sweet; he still had his pink cheeks.

"If you have your car, you can give me a lift," I said. Rahul is always a gentleman, and he even carried my bundle for me to his car.

It took us a long time to find the orphanage—it was right at the back of the Fatehpuri mosque somewhere—so there was plenty of time for me to talk to him. He listened quite quietly, driving the car through all that traffic. When at last we found the orphanage and I was ready to get out, he said, "Don't go yet." I stayed with him for a while, even though the car was parked very awkwardly in that crowded alley-way, and men with barrows swore at us because they could not get past.

Soon afterwards a friend of M.'s who was in the railways got transferred, and as he lived in a house with a very low rent, it was a good opportunity for us and we took it over from him. There were two rooms and a little yard at the back, and upstairs two families were living. Daddy used to send a cheque for the rent. I cooked for us and cleaned the house and talked with the families upstairs, while M. went out to see people about his ideas. But after a time he began to go out less and less, and he became depressed; he said the world had rejected him because he was not strong enough yet. Now it was his task to purify himself and make himself stronger. He stayed at home and meditated. A strange change came over him. Most of the time he sat in one of our rooms, in a corner of the floor, by himself and he wouldn't let me come in. Sometimes I heard him singing to himself and shouting—he made such strange noises, almost like an animal. For days he ate nothing at all and, when I tried to coax him, he upset the food I had brought and threw it on the floor. I tried to be patient and bear and understand everything.

His friends stopped coming and he hardly ever left that little room for two months. Then he started going out by himself—I never knew where and could not ask him. He had an expression on his face as if he were listening for something, so that one felt one couldn't disturb him. When he talked to me, he talked as if he was someone else and I was someone else. At night I slept in the yard at the back with the families from upstairs, who were always kind to me.

Then visitors began to come for him—not his old friends, but quite new people whom I had never seen before. They sat with him in the little room and I could hear him talking to them. At first only a few men used to come, but then more and more came, and women too. I also sat in the room sometimes and listened to him talk; he told strange stories about parrots and princes and tigers in the jungle, all of which had some deep meaning. When the people understood the deep meaning, they all exclaimed with pleasure and said God was speaking through his mouth.

Now they began to bring us gifts of food and money and clothes and even jewellery. M. never took any notice, and I just piled the things in the other room which was soon very crowded. We ate the food and I also gave it to the families upstairs, but there was still plenty left over, and at night someone used to come from the beggars' home to take it away. I sent a lot of money to Savitri. The house was always full of people now, and they spilled over into the yard and out into the street. More and more women came—

most of them were old but there were some young ones too, and the young ones were even more fervent and religious than the old ones. There was one plump and pretty young widow, who was always dressed very nicely and came every day. She said she was going mad with love of God and needed words of solace and comfort from M. She touched his feet and implored him to relieve her, and when he took no notice of her, she shook him and tugged at his clothes, so that he became quite angry.

Mama often came to see me. In the beginning she was very disgusted with the house and the way we lived and everything, but afterwards, when she saw how many people came and all the things they brought and how they respected M., she kept quiet on that subject. Now she only said, "Who knows what is to become of it all?" Mama is not really a religious person, but she has a lot of superstitions. When holy men come begging to her house, she always gives them something—not because of their holiness, but because she is afraid they will curse her and bring the evil eye on us all. She no longer said anything bad about M., and when she talked about him, she didn't say "that one" as she used to, but always "He." Once or twice she went and sat with the other people in the little room in which he was, and when she came out, she looked so grave and thoughtful that I had to laugh.

Rahul also visited me. At first he was stiff and sulky, as if he were doing me a favour by coming; but then he began to talk, all about how lonely he was and how his family were trying to persuade him to marry girls he didn't like. I felt sorry for him—I knew it is always difficult for him to make friends and he has never really had anyone except me. I let him talk, and he kept coming again and again. There was a little space with a roof of asbestos sheet over it in the yard, where I did my cooking, and it was here that Rahul and I sat. It was not a very private place because of all the people in the yard, waiting to see M., but Rahul soon got used to it and talked just as he would have done if we had been sitting in Mama's drawing-room. He was very melancholy, and when he had finished telling me about how lonely he was, he only sat and looked at me with big sad eyes. So I let him help me with the cooking—at first he only sifted the rice and lentils, but after a time I let him do some real cooking and he enjoyed it terribly. He would make all sorts of things—fritters and potato cakes and horse-radish pancakes—and they were really delicious. We ate some ourselves and the rest we sent to the beggars' home.

There were always a few young men who stayed at night and slept outside the door of the room where M. was. I often heard him get up in the night and walk up and down; and sometimes he shouted at the young men sleeping outside his door, "Go home!" and he kicked them with his foot, he was so impatient and angry with them. He was often angry nowadays. I heard him shouting at people and scolding them for coming to pester him. When he scolded them, they said he was right to do so, because they were bad, sinful people; but they did not go away and, on the contrary, even more came.

One night I felt someone shaking me to wake up. I opened my eyes and it was M. I jumped up at once and we went out into the street together and sat on a doorstep. Here and there people were sleeping on the sidewalk or on the platforms of shuttered shops. It was very dark and quiet.

Only sometimes someone coughed in his sleep or there was a watchman's cry and the tap of his stick. M. said, "Soon I shall have to go away."

Then I knew that the time I had always feared was near.

He said, "It will be best for you to go home again." He spoke very practically, and with gentleness and great concern for me.

But I didn't want to think about what I was going to do. For the moment I wanted it to be only now—always night and people always sleeping and he and I sitting together like this on the doorstep for ever and ever.

The plump young widow still came every day and every day in a different sari, and she made such scenes that in the end M. forbade her to come any more. So she hung about outside in the yard for a few days, and then she started peeping into his room and after that she crept in behind the others and sat quietly at the back; till finally she showed herself to him quite openly and even began to make scenes again. "Have pity!" she cried. "God is eating me up!" At last he quite lost his temper with her. He took off his slipper and began to beat her with it and when she ran away, screaming and clutching her sari about her, he ran after her, brandishing his slipper. They were a funny sight. He pursued her right out into the street, and then he turned back and began to chase all the other people out of the house. He scattered them right and left, beating at them with his slipper, and cursing and scolding. Everyone ran away very fast—even Rahul, who had been cooking potato cakes, made off in a great fright. When they had all gone, M. returned to his room and locked the door behind him. He looked hot and angry.

And next day he was gone. People came as usual that day but when they realized he was no longer there, they went away again and also took their gifts back with them. That night the men from the beggars' home were disappointed. I stayed on by myself, it didn't matter to me where I was. Sometimes I sat in one of the rooms, sometimes I walked up and down. The families from upstairs tried to make me eat and sleep, but I heard nothing of what they said. I don't remember much about that time. Later Daddy came to take me away. For the last time I tied my things up in a sheet and I went with him.

I think sometimes of Savitri, and I wonder whether I too am like her now—a candle burning for him in a window of the world. I am patient and inwardly calm and lead the life that has been appointed for me. I play tennis again and I go out to tea and garden-parties with Mama, and Rahul and I often dance to the gramophone. Probably I shall marry Rahul quite soon. I laugh and talk just as much as I used to and Mama says I am too frivolous, but Daddy smiles and encourages me. Mama has had a lot of new pieces of jewellery made for me to replace the ones I sold; she and I keep on quarrelling as before.

I still try and see his face in my mind, and I never succeed. But I know—and that is how I can go on living the way I do, and even enjoy my life and be glad—that one day I shall succeed and I shall see that face as it really is. But whose face it is I shall see in that hour of happiness—and indeed, whose face it is I look for with such longing—is not quite clear to me.

EDNA O'BRIEN

Irish Revel

Mary hoped that the rotted front tire would not burst. As it was, the tube had a slow puncture, and twice she had to stop and use the pump, maddening, because the pump had no connection and had to be jammed on over the corner of a handkerchief. For as long as she could remember she had been pumping bicycles, carting turf, cleaning outhouses, doing a man's work. Her father and her two brothers worked for the forestry, so that she and her mother had to do all the odd jobs—there were three children to care for, and fowl and pigs and churning. Theirs was a mountainy farm in Ireland, and life was hard.

But this cold evening in early November she was free. She rode along the mountain road, between the bare thorn hedges, thinking pleasantly about the party. Although she was seventeen this was her first party. The invitation had come only that morning from Mrs. Rodgers of the Commercial Hotel. The postman brought word that Mrs. Rodgers wanted her down that evening, without fail. At first, her mother did not wish Mary to go, there was too much to be done, gruel to be made, and one of the twins had an earache, and was likely to cry in the night. Mary slept with the year-old twins, and sometimes she was afraid that she might lie on them or smother them, the bed was so small. She begged to be let go.

"What use would it be?" her mother said. To her mother all outings were unsettling—they gave you a taste of something you couldn't have. But finally she weakened, mainly because Mrs. Rodgers, as owner of the Commercial Hotel, was an important woman, and not to be insulted.

"You can go, so long as you're back in time for the milking in the morning; and mind you don't lose your head," her mother warned. Mary was to stay overnight in the village with Mrs. Rodgers. She plaited her hair, and later when she combed it it fell in dark crinkled waves over her shoulders. She was allowed to wear the black lace dress that had come from America years ago and belonged to no one in particular. Her mother had sprinkled her with Holy Water, conveyed her to the top of the lane, and warned her never to touch alcohol.

Mary felt happy as she rode along slowly, avoiding the potholes that were thinly iced over. The frost had never lifted that day. The ground was hard. If it went on like that, the cattle would have to be brought into the shed and given hay.

The road turned and looped and rose; she turned and looped with it, climbing little hills and descending again toward the next hill. At the descent of the Big Hill she got off the bicycle—the brakes were unreliable—and looked back, out of habit, at her own house. It was the only house back there on the mountain, small, whitewashed, with a few trees around it, and a patch at the back which they called a kitchen garden. There was a rhubarb bed, and shrubs over which they emptied tea leaves, and a stretch of grass where in the summer they had a chicken run, moving it from one patch to the next, every other day. She looked away. She was now free to think of John Roland. He came to their district two years before, riding a motorcycle at a ferocious speed; raising dust on the milk cloths spread on the hedge to dry. He stopped to ask the way. He was staying with Mrs. Rodgers in the Commercial Hotel and had come up to see the lake, which was noted for its colors. It changed color rapidly—it was blue and green and black, all within an hour. At sunset it was often a strange burgundy, not like a lake at all, but like wine.

"Down there," she said to the stranger, pointing to the lake below, with the small island in the middle of it. He had taken a wrong turning.

Hills and tiny cornfields descended steeply toward the water. The misery of the hills was clear, from all the boulders. The cornfields were turning, it was midsummer; the ditches throbbing with the blood-red of fuchsia; the milk sour five hours after it had been put in the tanker. He said how exotic it was. She had no interest in views herself. She just looked up at the high sky and saw that a hawk had halted in the air above them. It was like a pause in her life, the hawk above them, perfectly still; and just then her mother came out to see who the stranger was. He took off his helmet and said "Hello," very courteously. He introduced himself as John Roland, an English painter, who lived in Italy.

She did not remember exactly how it happened, but after a while he walked into their kitchen with them and sat down to tea.

Two long years since; but she had never given up hoping —perhaps this evening. The mail-car man said that someone special in the Commercial Hotel expected her. She felt such happiness. She spoke to her bicycle, and it seemed to her that her happiness somehow glowed in the pearliness of the cold sky, in the frosted fields going blue in the dusk, in the cottage windows she passed. Her father and mother were rich and cheerful; the twin had no earache; the kitchen fire did not smoke. Now and then, she smiled at the thought of how she would appear to him—taller and with breasts now, and a dress that could be worn anywhere. She forgot about the rotted tire, got up and cycled.

The five street lights were on when she pedaled into the village. There had been a cattle fair that day, and the main street was covered with dung. The townspeople had their windows protected with wooden half-shutters and make-shift arrangements of planks and barrels. Some were out scrubbing their own piece of footpath with bucket and brush. There were cattle wandering around, mooing, the way cattle do when they are in a strange street, and drunken farmers with sticks were trying to identify their own cattle in dark corners.

Beyond the shop window of the Commercial Hotel, Mary heard loud conversation, and men singing. It was opaque glass so that she could not identify any of them, she could just see their heads moving about, inside. It was a shabby hotel; the yellow-washed walls needed a coat of paint, as they hadn't been done since the time De Valera came to that village during the election campaign five years before. De Valera went upstairs that time, and sat in the parlor and wrote his name with a penny pen in an autograph book, and sympathized with Mrs. Rodgers on the recent death of her husband.

Mary thought of resting her bicycle against the porter barrels under the shop window, and then of climbing the three stone steps that led to the hall door, but suddenly the latch of the shop door clicked and she ran in terror up the alley by the side of the shop, afraid it might be someone who knew her father and would say he saw her going in through the public bar. She wheeled her bicycle into a shed and approached the back door. It was open, but she did not enter without knocking.

Two townsgirls rushed to answer it. One was Doris O'Beirne, the daughter of the harnessmaker. She was the only Doris in the whole village, and she was famous for that, as well as for the fact that one of her eyes was blue and the other a dark brown. She learnt shorthand and typing at the local technical school, and later she meant to be a secretary to some famous man or other in the Government, in Dublin.

"God, I thought it was someone important," she said when she saw Mary standing there, blushing, pretty, and with a bottle of cream in her hand. Another girl! Girls were two a penny in that neighborhood. People said that it had something to do with the lime water that so many girls were born. Girls with pink skins, and matching eyes, and girls like Mary with long, wavy hair and good figures.

"Come in, or stay out," said Eithne Duggan, the second girl, to Mary. It was supposed to be a joke but neither of them liked her. They hated mountainy people.

Mary came in carrying the cream, which her mother had sent to Mrs. Rodgers, as a present. She put it on the dresser and took off her coat. The girls nudged each other when they saw her dress. In the kitchen was a smell of cow dung and fried onions.

"Where's Mrs. Rodgers?" Mary asked.

"Serving," Doris said in a saucy voice, as if any fool ought to know. Two old men sat at the table eating.

"I can't chew, I have no teeth," said one of the men, to Doris. " 'Tis like leather," he said, holding the plate of burnt steak toward her. He had watery eyes and he blinked childishly. Was it so, Mary wondered, that eyes got paler with age, like bluebells in a jar?

"You're not going to charge me for that," the old man was saying to Doris. Tea and steak cost five shillings at the Commercial.

" 'Tis good for you, chewing is," Eithne Duggan said, teasing him.

"I can't chew with my gums," he said again, and the two girls began to giggle. The old man looked pleased that he had made them laugh, and he closed his mouth and munched once or twice on a piece of fresh shop bread. Eithne Duggan laughed so much that she had to put a dishcloth between her teeth. Mary took off her coat and went through to the shop.

Mrs. Rodgers came from the counter for a moment to speak to her.

"Mary, I'm glad you came, that pair in there are no use at all, always giggling. Now first thing we have to do is to get the parlor upstairs straightened out. Everything has to come out of it except the piano. We're going to have dancing and everything."

Quickly, Mary realized that she was being given work to do, and she blushed with shock and disappointment.

"Pitch everything into the back bedroom, the whole shootin' lot," Mrs. Rodgers was saying as Mary thought of her good lace dress, and of how her mother wouldn't even let her wear it to Mass on Sundays.

"And we have to stuff a goose too and get it on," Mrs. Rodgers said, and went on to explain that the party was in honor of the local Customs and Excise Officer who was retiring because his wife won some money in the Sweep. Two thousand pounds. His wife lived thirty miles away at the far side of Limerick and he lodged in the Commercial Hotel from Monday to Friday, going home for the weekends.

"There's someone here expecting me," Mary said, trembling with the pleasure of being about to hear his name pronounced by someone else. She wondered which room was his, and if he was likely to be in at that moment. Already in imagination she had climbed the rickety stairs and knocked on the door, and heard him move around inside.

"Expecting you!" Mrs. Rodgers said, and looked puzzled for a minute. "Oh, that lad from the slate quarry was inquiring about you, he said he saw you at a dance once. He's as odd as two left shoes."

"What lad?" Mary said, as she felt the joy leaking out of her heart.

"Oh, what's his name?" Mrs. Rodgers said, and then to the men with empty glasses who were shouting for her. "Oh, all right, I'm coming."

Upstairs Doris and Eithne helped Mary move the heavy pieces of furniture. They dragged the sideboard across the landing and one of the castors tore the linoleum. She was expiring, because she had the heaviest end, the other two being at the same side. She felt that it was on purpose: they ate sweets without offering her one, and she caught them making faces at her dress. The dress worried her too, in case anything should happen to it. If one of the lace threads caught in a splinter of wood, or on a porter barrel, she would have no business going home in the morning. They carried out a varnished bamboo whatnot, a small table, knickknacks, and a chamberpot with no handle which held some withered hydrangeas. They smelt awful.

"How much is the doggie in the window, the one with the waggledy tail?" Doris O'Beirne sang to a white china dog and swore that there wasn't ten pounds' worth of furniture in the whole shibeen.

"Are you leaving your curlers in, Dot, till it starts?" Eithne Duggan asked her friend.

"Oh def.," Doris O'Beirne said. She wore an assortment of curlers—white pipe cleaners, metal clips, and pink, plastic rollers. Eithne had just taken hers out and her hair, dyed blonde, stood out, all frizzed and alarming. She reminded Mary of a moulting hen about to attempt flight. She was, God bless her, an unfortunate girl with a squint, jumbled teeth, and almost no lips; like something put together hurriedly. That was the luck of the draw.

"Take these," Doris O'Beirne said, handing Mary bunches of yellowed bills crammed on skewers.

Do this! Do that! They ordered her around like a maid. She dusted the piano, top and sides, and the yellow and black keys; then the surround, and the wainscoting. The dust, thick on everything, had settled into a hard film because of the damp in that room. A party! She'd have been as well off at home, at least it was clean dirt attending to calves and pigs and the like.

Doris and Eithne amused themselves, hitting notes on the piano at random and wandering from one mirror to the next. There were two mirrors in the parlor and one side of the folding fire screen was a blotchy mirror too. The other two sides were of water lilies painted on black cloth, but like everything else in the room it was old.

"What's that?" Doris and Eithne asked each other, as they heard a hullaballoo downstairs. They rushed out to see what it was and Mary followed. Over the banisters they saw that a young bullock had got in the hall door and was slithering over the tiled floor, trying to find his way out again.

"Don't excite her, don't excite her, I tell ye," said the old, toothless man to the young boy who tried to drive the black bullock out. Two more boys were having a bet as to whether or not the bullock would do something on the floor when Mrs. Rodgers came out and dropped a glass of porter. The beast backed out the way he'd come, shaking his head from side to side.

Eithne and Doris clasped each other in laughter and then Doris drew back so that none of the boys would see her in her curling pins and call her names. Mary had gone back to the room, downcast. Wearily she pushed the chairs back against the wall and swept the linoleumed floor where they were later to dance.

"She's bawling in there," Eithne Duggan told her friend Doris. They had locked themselves into the bathroom with a bottle of cider.

"God, she's a right-looking eejit in the dress," Doris said. "And the length of it!"

"It's her mother's," Eithne said. She had admired the dress before that, when Doris was out of the room, and had asked Mary where she bought it.

"What's she crying about?" Doris wondered, aloud.

"She thought some lad would be here. Do you remember that lad stayed here the summer before last and had a motorcycle?"

"He was a Jew," Doris said. "You could tell by his nose. God, she'd shake him in that dress, he'd think she was a scarecrow." She squeezed a blackhead on her chin, tightened a curling pin which had come loose and said, "Her hair isn't natural either, you can see it's curled."

"I hate that kind of black hair, it's like a gypsy's," Eithne said, drinking the last of the cider. They hid the bottle under the scoured bath.

"Have a cachou, take the smell off your breath," Doris

said as she hawed on the bathroom mirror and wondered if she would get off with that fellow O'Toole, from the slate quarry, who was coming to the party.

In the front room Mary polished glasses. Tears ran down her cheeks so she did not put on the light. She foresaw how the party would be; they would all stand around and consume the goose, which was now simmering in the turf range. The men would be drunk, the girls giggling. Having eaten, they would dance, and sing, and tell ghost stories, and in the morning she would have to get up early and be home in time to milk. She moved toward the dark pane of window with a glass in her hand and looked out at the dirtied streets, remembering how once she had danced with John on the upper road to no music at all, just their hearts beating, and the sound of happiness.

He came into their house for tea that summer's day and on her father's suggestion he lodged with them for four days, helping with the hay and oiling all the farm machinery for her father. He understood machinery. He put back doorknobs that had fallen off. Mary made his bed in the daytime and carried up a ewer of water from the rain barrel every evening, so that he could wash. She washed the check shirt he wore, and that day, his bare back peeled in the sun. She put milk on it. It was his last day with them. After supper he proposed giving each of the grown-up children a ride on the motorcycle. Her turn came last, she felt that he had planned it that way, but it may have been that her brothers were more persistent about being first. She would never forget that ride. She warmed from head to foot in wonder and joy. He praised her as a good balancer and at odd moments he took one hand off the handlebar and gave her clasped hands a comforting pat. The sun went down, and the gorse flowers blazed yellow. They did not talk for miles; she had his stomach encased in the delicate and frantic grasp of a girl in love and no matter how far they rode they seemed always to be riding into a golden haze. He saw the lake at its most glorious. They got off at the bridge five miles away, and sat on the limestone wall that was cushioned by moss and lichen. She took a tick out of his neck and touched the spot where the tick had drawn one pinprick of blood; it was then they danced. A sound of larks and running water. The hay in the fields was lying green and ungathered, and the air was sweet with the smell of it. They danced.

"Sweet Mary," he said, looking earnestly into her eyes. Her eyes were a greenish-brown. He confessed that he could not love her, because he already loved his wife and children, and anyhow he said, "You are too young and too innocent."

Next day, as he was leaving, he asked if he might send her something in the post, and it came eleven days later: a black-and-white drawing of her, very like her, except that the girl in the drawing was uglier.

"A fat lot of good, that is," said her mother, who had been expecting a gold bracelet or a brooch. "That wouldn't take you far."

They hung it on a nail in the kitchen for a while and then one day it fell down and someone (probably her mother) used it to sweep dust on to, ever since it was used for that purpose. Mary had wanted to keep it, to put it away in a trunk, but she was ashamed to. They were hard people, and it was only when someone died that they could give in to sentiment or crying.

"Sweet Mary," he had said. He never wrote. Two summers passed, devil's pokers flowered for two seasons, and thistle seed blew in the wind, the trees in the forestry were a foot higher. She had a feeling that he would come back, and a gnawing fear that he might not.

• • •

> *"OH it ain't gonna rain no more, no more,*
> *it ain't gonna rain no more;*
> *How in the hell can the old folks say*
> *it ain't gonna rain no more."*

So sang Brogan, whose party it was, in the upstairs room of the Commercial Hotel. Unbuttoning his brown waistcoat, he sat back and said what a fine spread it was. They had carried the goose up on a platter and it lay in the center of the mahogany table with potato stuffing spilling out of it. There were sausages also and polished glasses rim downward, and plates and forks for everyone.

"A fork supper" was how Mrs. Rodgers described it. She had read about it in the paper; it was all the rage now in posh houses in Dublin, this fork supper where you stood up for your food and ate with a fork only. Mary had brought knives in case anyone got into difficulties.

" 'Tis America at home," Hickey said, putting turf on the smoking fire.

The pub door was bolted downstairs, the shutters across, as the eight guests upstairs watched Mrs. Rodgers carve the goose and then tear the loose pieces away with her fingers. Every so often she wiped her fingers on a tea towel.

"Here you are, Mary, give this to Mr. Brogan, as he's the guest of honor." Mr. Brogan got a lot of breast and some crispy skin as well.

"Don't forget the sausages, Mary," Mrs. Rodgers said. Mary had to do everything, pass the food around, serve the stuffing, ask people whether they wanted paper plates or china ones. Mrs. Rodgers had bought paper plates, thinking they were sophisticated.

"I could eat a young child," Hickey said.

Mary was surprised that people in towns were so coarse and outspoken. When he squeezed her finger she did not smile at all. She wished that she were at home—she knew what they were doing at home; the boys at their lessons; her mother baking a cake of wholemeal bread, because there was never enough time during the day to bake; her father rolling cigarettes and talking to himself. John had taught him how to roll cigarettes, and every night since he rolled four and smoked four. He was a good man, her father, but dour. In another hour they'd be saying the Rosary in her house and going up to bed: the rhythm of their lives never changed, the fresh bread was always cool by morning.

"Ten o'clock," Doris said, listening to the chimes of the landing clock.

The party began late; the men were late getting back from the dogs in Limerick. They killed a pig on the way in their anxiety to get back quickly. The pig had been wandering around the road and the car came round the corner; it got run over instantly.

"Never heard such a roarin' in all me born days," Hickey said, reaching for a wing of goose, the choicest bit.

"We should have brought it with us," O'Toole said. O'Toole worked in the slate quarry and knew nothing about pigs or farming; he was tall and thin and jagged. He had bright green eyes and a face like a greyhound; his hair was so gold that it looked dyed, but in fact it was bleached by the weather. No one had offered him any food.

"A nice way to treat a man," he said.

"God bless us, Mary, didn't you give Mr. O'Toole anything to eat yet?" Mrs. Rodgers said as she thumped Mary on the back to hurry her up. Mary brought him a large helping on a paper plate and he thanked her and said that they would dance later. To him she looked far prettier than those good-for-nothing townsgirls—she was tall and thin like himself; she had long black hair that some people might think streelish, but not him, he liked long hair and simple-minded girls; maybe later on he'd get her to go into one of the other rooms where they could do it. She had funny eyes when you looked into them, brown and deep, like a bloody bog hole.

"Have a wish," he said to her as he held the wishbone up. She wished that she were going to America on an airplane and on second thought she wished that she would win a lot of money and could buy her mother and father a house near the main road.

"Is that your brother the Bishop?" Eithne Duggan, who knew well that it was, asked Mrs. Rodgers, concerning the flaccid-faced cleric over the fireplace. Unknown to herself Mary had traced the letter J on the dust of the picture mirror, earlier on, and now they all seemed to be looking at it, knowing how it came to be there.

"That's him, poor Charlie," Mrs. Rodgers said proudly, and was about to elaborate, but Brogan began to sing, unexpectedly.

"Let the man sing, can't you," O'Toole said, hushing two of the girls who were having a joke about the armchair they shared; the springs were hanging down underneath and the girls said that any minute the whole thing would collapse.

Mary shivered in her lace dress. The air was cold and damp even though Hickey had got up a good fire. There hadn't been a fire in that room since the day De Valera signed the autograph book. Steam issued from everything.

O'Toole asked if any of the ladies would care to sing. There were five ladies in all—Mrs. Rodgers, Mary, Doris, Eithne, and Crystal the local hairdresser, who had a new red rinse in her hair and who insisted that the food was a little heavy for her. The goose was greasy and undercooked, she did not like its raw, pink color. She liked dainty things, little bits of cold chicken breast with sweet pickles. Her real name was Carmel, but when she started up as a hairdresser she changed to Crystal and dyed her brown hair red.

"I bet you can sing," O'Toole said to Mary.

"Where she comes from they can hardly talk," Doris said.

Mary felt the blood rushing to her sallow cheeks. She would not tell them, but her father's name had been in the paper once, because he had seen a pine marten in the forestry plantation; and they ate with a knife and fork at home and had oilcloth on the kitchen table, and kept a tin of coffee in case strangers called. She would not tell them anything. She just hung her head, making clear that she was not about to sing.

In honor of the Bishop, O'Toole put "Far Away in Australia" on the horn gramophone. Mrs. Rodgers had asked for it. The sound issued forth with rasps and scratchings and Brogan said he could do better than that himself.

"Christ, lads, we forgot the soup!" Mrs. Rodgers said suddenly, as she threw down the fork and went toward the door. There had been soup scheduled to begin with.

"I'll help you," Doris O'Beirne said, stirring herself for the first time that night, and they both went down to get the pot of dark giblet soup which had been simmering all that day.

"Now we need two pounds from each of the gents," said O'Toole, taking the opportunity while Mrs. Rodgers was away to mention the delicate matter of money. The men had agreed to pay two pounds each, to cover the cost of the drink; the ladies did not have to pay anything, but were invited so as to lend a pleasant and decorative atmosphere to the party, and, of course, to help.

O'Toole went around with his cap held out, and Brogan said that as it was *his* party he ought to give a fiver.

"I ought to give a fiver, but I suppose ye wouldn't hear of that," Brogan said, and handed up two pound notes. Hickey paid up too, and O'Toole himself and Long John Salmon—who was silent up to then. O'Toole gave it to Mrs. Rodgers when she returned and told her to clock it up against the damages.

"Sure that's too kind altogether," she said, as she put it behind the stuffed owl on the mantelpiece, under the Bishop's watchful eye.

She served the soup in cups and Mary was asked to pass the cups around. The grease floated like drops of molten gold on the surface of each cup.

"See you later, alligator," Hickey said, as she gave him his; then he asked her for a piece of bread because he wasn't used to soup without bread.

"Tell us, Brogan," said Hickey to his rich friend, "what'll you do, now that you're a rich man?"

"Oh go on, tell us," said Doris O'Beirne.

"Well," said Brogan, thinking for a minute, "we're going to make some changes at home." None of them had ever visited Brogan's home because it was situated in Adare, thirty miles away, at the far side of Limerick. None of them had ever seen his wife either, who it seems lived there and kept bees.

"What sort of changes?" someone said.

"We're going to do up the drawing room, and we're going to have flower beds," Brogan told them.

"And what else?" Crystal asked, thinking of all the lovely clothes she could buy with that money, clothes and jewelry.

"Well," said Brogan, thinking again, "we might even go to Lourdes. I'm not sure yet, it all depends."

"I'd give my two eyes to go to Lourdes," Mrs. Rodgers said.

"And you'd get 'em back when you arrived there," Hickey said, but no one paid any attention to him.

O'Toole filled out four half-tumblers of whisky and

then stood back to examine the glasses to see that each one had the same amount. There was always great anxiety among the men, about being fair with drink. Then O'Toole stood bottles of stout in little groups of six and told each man which group was his. The ladies had gin and orange.

"Orange for me," Mary said, but O'Toole told her not to be such a goody, and when her back was turned he put gin in her orange.

They drank a toast to Brogan.

"To Lourdes," Mrs. Rogers said.

"To Brogan," O'Toole said.

"To myself," Hickey said.

"Mud in your eye," said Doris O'Beirne, who was already unsteady from tippling cider.

"Well we're not sure about Lourdes," Brogan said. "But we'll get the drawing room done up anyhow, and the flower beds put in."

"We've a drawing room here," Mrs. Rodgers said, "and no one ever sets foot in it."

"Come into the drawing room, Doris," said O'Toole to Mary, who was serving the jelly from the big enamel basin. They'd had no china bowl to put it in. It was red jelly with whipped egg white in it, but something went wrong because it hadn't set properly. She served it in saucers, and thought to herself what a rough-and-ready party it was. There wasn't a proper cloth on the table either, just a plastic one, and no napkins, and that big basin with the jelly in it. Maybe people washed in that basin, downstairs.

"Well, someone tell us a bloomin' joke," said Hickey,

who was getting fed up with talk about drawing rooms and flower beds.

"I'll tell you a joke," said Long John Salmon, erupting out of his silence.

"Good," said Brogan, as he sipped from his whisky glass and his stout glass alternately. It was the only way to drink enjoyably. That was why, in pubs, he was much happier if he could buy his own drink and not rely on anyone else's meanness.

"Is it a funny joke?" Hickey asked of Long John Salmon.

"It's about my brother," said Long John Salmon, "my brother Patrick."

"Oh no, don't tell us that old rambling thing again," said Hickey and O'Toole, together.

"Oh let him tell it," said Mrs. Rodgers, who'd never heard the story before.

Long John Salmon began, "I had this brother Patrick and he died; the heart wasn't too good."

"Holy Christ, not this again," said Brogan, recollecting which story it was.

But Long John Salmon went on, undeterred by the abuse from the three men:

"One day I was standing in the shed, about a month after he was buried, and I saw him coming out of the wall, walking across the yard."

"Oh what would you do if you saw a thing like that," Doris said to Eithne.

"Let him tell it," Mrs. Rodgers said. "Go on, Long John."

"Well it was walking toward me, and I said to myself, 'What do I do now?'; 'twas raining heavy, so I said to my brother Patrick, 'Stand in out of the wet or you'll get drenched.' "

"And then?" said one of the girls anxiously.

"He vanished," said Long John Salmon.

"Ah God, let us have a bit of music," said Hickey, who had heard that story nine or ten times. It had neither a beginning, a middle, or an end. They put a record on, and O'Toole asked Mary to dance. He did a lot of fancy steps and capering; and now and then he let out a mad "Yippee." Brogan and Mrs. Rodgers were dancing too and Crystal said that she'd dance if anyone asked her.

"Come on, knees up, Mother Brown," O'Toole said to Mary, as he jumped around the room, kicking the legs of chairs as he moved. She felt funny: her head was swaying round and round, and in the pit of her stomach there was a nice, ticklish feeling that made her want to lie back and stretch her legs. A new feeling that frightened her.

"Come into the drawing room, Doris," he said, dancing her right out of the room and into the cold passage where he kissed her clumsily.

Inside, Crystal O'Meara had begun to cry. That was how drink affected her; either she cried or talked in a foreign accent and said, "Why am I talking in a foreign accent?" This time she cried.

"Hickey, there is no joy in life," she said at the table with her head laid in her arms and her blouse slipping up out of her skirtband.

"What joy?" said Hickey, who had all the drink he needed, and a pound note which he slipped from behind the owl when no one was looking.

Doris and Eithne sat on either side of Long John Salmon,

asking if they could go out next year when the sugar plums were ripe. Long John Salmon lived by himself, way up the country, and he had a big orchard. He was odd and silent in himself; he took a swim every day, winter and summer, in the river, at the back of his house.

"Two old married people," Brogan said, as he put his arm around Mrs. Rodgers and urged her to sit down because he was out of breath from dancing. He said he'd go away with happy memories of them all, and sitting down he drew her on to his lap. She was a heavy woman, with straggly brown hair that had once been a nut color.

"There is no joy in life," Crystal sobbed, as the gramophone made crackling noises and Mary ran in from the landing, away from O'Toole.

"I mean business," O'Toole said, and winked.

O'Toole was the first to get quarrelsome.

"Now ladies, now gentlemen, a little laughing sketch, are we ready?" he asked.

"Fire ahead," Hickey told him.

"Well, there was these three lads, Paddy th'Irishman, Paddy th'Englishman, and Paddy the Scotsman, and they were badly in need of a . . ."

"Now, no smut," Mrs. Rodgers snapped, before he had uttered a wrong word at all.

"What smut?" said O'Toole, getting offended. "Smut!" And he asked her to explain an accusation like that.

"Think of the girls," Mrs. Rodgers said.

"Girls," O'Toole sneered, as he picked up the bottle of cream—which they'd forgotten to use with the jelly—and poured it into the carcass of the ravaged goose.

"Christ's sake, man," Hickey said, taking the bottle of cream out of O'Toole's hand.

Mrs. Rodgers said that it was high time everyone went to bed, as the party seemed to be over.

The guests would spend the night in the Commercial. It was too late for them to go home anyhow, and also Mrs. Rodgers did not want them to be observed staggering out of the house at that hour. The police watched her like hawks and she didn't want any trouble, until Christmas was over at least. The sleeping arrangements had been decided earlier on—there were three bedrooms vacant. One was Brogan's, the room he always slept in. The other three men were to pitch in together in the second big bedroom, and the girls were to share the back room with Mrs. Rodgers herself.

"Come on, everyone, blanket street," Mrs. Rodgers said, as she put a guard in front of the dying fire and took the money from behind the owl.

"Sugar you," O'Toole said, pouring stout now into the carcass of the goose, and Long John Salmon wished that he had never come. He thought of daylight and of his swim in the mountain river at the back of his gray stone house.

"Ablution," he said, aloud, taking pleasure in the word and in thought of the cold water touching him. He could do without people, people were waste. He remembered catkins on a tree outside his window, catkins in February as white as snow; who needed people?

"Crystal, stir yourself," Hickey said, as he put on her shoes and patted the calves of her legs.

Brogan kissed the four girls and saw them across the

landing to the bedroom. Mary was glad to escape without O'Toole noticing; he was very obstreperous and Hickey was trying to control him.

In the bedroom she sighed; she had forgotten all about the furniture being pitched in there. Wearily they began to unload the things. The room was so crammed that they could hardly move in it. Mary suddenly felt alert and frightened, because O'Toole could be heard yelling and singing out on the landing. There had been gin in her orangeade, she knew now, because she breathed closely onto the palm of her hand and smelled her own breath. She had broken her Confirmation pledge, broken her promise; it would bring her bad luck.

Mrs. Rodgers came in and said that five of them would be too crushed in the bed, so that she herself would sleep on the sofa for one night.

"Two of you at the top and two at the bottom," she said, as she warned them not to break any of the ornaments, and not to stay talking all night.

"Night and God Bless," she said, as she shut the door behind her.

"Nice thing," said Doris O'Beirne, "bunging us all in here; I wonder where she's off to?"

"Will you loan me curlers?" Crystal asked. To Crystal, hair was the most important thing on earth. She would never get married because you couldn't wear curlers in bed then. Eithne Duggan said she wouldn't put curlers in now if she got five million for doing it, she was that jaded. She threw herself down on the quilt and spread her arms out. She was a noisy, sweaty girl but Mary liked her better than the other two.

"Ah me old segotums," O'Toole said, pushing their door in. The girls exclaimed and asked him to go out at once as they were preparing for bed.

"Come into the drawing room, Doris," he said to Mary, and curled his forefinger at her. He was drunk and couldn't focus her properly but he knew that she was standing there somewhere.

"Go to bed, you're drunk," Doris O'Beirne said, and he stood very upright for an instant and asked her to speak for herself.

"Go to bed, Michael, you're tired," Mary said to him. She tried to sound calm because he looked so wild.

"Come into the drawing room, I tell you," he said, as he caught her wrist and dragged her toward the door. She let out a cry, and Eithne Duggan said she'd brain him if he didn't leave the girl alone.

"Give me that flower pot, Doris," Eithne Duggan called, and then Mary began to cry in case there might be a scene. She hated scenes. Once she heard her father and a neighbor having a row about boundary rights and she'd never forgotten it; they both had been a bit drunk, after a fair.

"Are you cracked or are you mad?" O'Toole said when he perceived that she was crying.

"I'll give you two seconds," Eithne warned, as she held the flower pot high, ready to throw it at O'Toole's stupefied face.

"You're a nice bunch of hard-faced aul crows, crows," he said. "Wouldn't give a man a squeeze," and he went out cursing each one of them. They shut the door very quickly and dragged the sideboard in front of the door so that he could not break in when they were asleep.

They got into bed in their underwear; Mary and Eithne at one end with Crystal's feet between their faces.

"You have lovely hair," Eithne whispered to Mary. It was the nicest thing she could think of to say. They each said their prayers, and shook hands under the covers and settled down to sleep.

"Hey," Doris O'Beirne said a few seconds later, "I never went to the lav."

"You can't go now," Eithne said, "the sideboard's in front of the door."

"I'll die if I don't go," Doris O'Beirne said.

"And me, too, after all that orange we drank," Crystal said. Mary was shocked that they could talk like that. At home you never spoke of such a thing, you just went out behind the hedge and that was that. Once a workman saw her squatting down and from that day she never talked to him, or acknowledged that she knew him.

"Maybe we could use that old pot," Doris O'Beirne said, and Eithne Duggan sat up and said that if anyone used a pot in that room she wasn't going to sleep there.

"We have to use something," Doris said. By now she had got up and had switched on the light. She held the pot up to the naked bulb and saw what looked to be a hole in it.

"Try it," Crystal said, giggling.

They heard feet on the landing and then the sound of choking and coughing, and later O'Toole cursing and swearing and hitting the wall with his fist. Mary curled down under the clothes, thankful for the company of the girls. They stopped talking.

"I was at a party. Now I know what parties are like,"

Mary said to herself, as she tried to force herself asleep. She heard a sound as of water running, but it did not seem to be raining outside. Later, she dozed, but at daybreak she heard the hall door bang, and she sat up in bed abruptly. She had to be home early to milk, so she got up, took her shoes and her lace dress, and let herself out by dragging the sideboard forward, and opening the door slightly.

There were newspapers spread on the landing floor and in the lavatory, and a heavy smell pervaded. Downstairs, porter had flowed out of the bar into the hall. It was probably O'Toole who had turned on the taps of the five porter barrels, and the stone-floored bar and sunken passage outside was swimming with black porter. Mrs. Rodgers would kill somebody. Mary put on her high-heeled shoes and picked her steps carefully across the room to the door. She left without even making a cup of tea.

She wheeled her bicycle down the alley and into the street. The front tire was dead flat. She pumped for half an hour but it remained flat.

The frost lay like a spell upon the street, upon the sleeping windows, and the slate roofs of the narrow houses. It had magically made the dunged street white and clean. She did not feel tired, but relieved to be out, and stunned by lack of sleep she inhaled the beauty of the morning. She walked briskly, sometimes looking back to see the track which her bicycle and her feet made on the white road.

Mrs. Rodgers wakened at eight and stumbled out in

her big nightgown from Brogan's warm bed. She smelt disaster instantly and hurried downstairs to find the porter in the bar and the hall; then she ran to call the others.

"Porter all over the place; every drop of drink in the house is on the floor—Mary Mother of God help me in my tribulation! Get up, get up." She rapped on their door and called the girls by name.

The girls rubbed their sleepy eyes, yawned, and sat up.

"She's gone," Eithne said, looking at the place on the pillow where Mary's head had been.

"Oh, a sneaky country one," Doris said, as she got into her taffeta dress and went down to see the flood. "If I have to clean that, in my good clothes, I'll die," she said. But Mrs. Rodgers had already brought brushes and pails and got to work. They opened the bar door and began to bail the porter into the street. Dogs came to lap it up, and Hickey, who had by then come down, stood and said what a crying shame it was, to waste all that drink. Outside it washed away an area of frost and revealed the dung of yesterday's fair day. O'Toole the culprit had fled since the night; Long John Salmon was gone for his swim, and upstairs in bed Brogan snuggled down for a last-minute heat and deliberated on the joys that he would miss when he left the Commercial for good.

"And where's my lady with the lace dress?" Hickey asked, recalling very little of Mary's face, but distinctly remembering the sleeves of her black dress which dipped into the plates.

"Sneaked off, before we were up," Doris said. They all agreed that Mary was no bloody use and should never have been asked.

"And 'twas she set O'Toole mad, egging him on and then disappointing him," Doris said, and Mrs. Rodgers swore that O'Toole, or Mary's father, or someone, would pay dear for the wasted drink.

"I suppose she's home by now," Hickey said, as he rooted in his pocket for a butt. He had a new packet, but if he produced that they'd all be puffing away at his expense.

Mary was half a mile from home, sitting on a bank.

If only I had a sweetheart, something to hold on to, she thought, as she cracked some ice with her high heel and watched the crazy splintered pattern it made. The poor birds could get no food, as the ground was frozen hard. Frost was general all over Ireland; frost like a weird blossom on the branches, on the riverbank from which Long John Salmon leaped in his great, hairy nakedness, on the ploughs left out all winter; frost on the stony fields, and on all the slime and ugliness of the world.

Walking again she wondered if and what she would tell her mother and her brothers about it, and if all parties were as bad. She was at the top of the hill now, and could see her own house, like a little white box at the end of the world, waiting to receive her.

Your Body Is a Jewel Box

I

The rain was falling just as it did every day at this time of the year, great handfuls of it flung hard on the windows, and when Olive got out of bed she saw that Mildred was sitting on the roof again, holding her knees in her bare arms and crying in the rain.

"For heaven's sake," said Olive, opening the window, "come in, Mildred. Don't sit there like that. Come in, now, do," she said, reaching her hand out to her sister. The two of them were in their nightgowns still, the dark girl on the roof and the yellow-haired girl standing inside the bedroom. "Come in now, Mildred, and we'll go down to the fire and get dry."

But Mildred only raised her head from her arms and looked in what might have been grief at her sister. But in spite of the tears that ran out of her eyes, it was not grief, for there was no look of sorrow in her face; only the black inhuman look of a wounded beast, even in pain, the small, suspicious, weary eye. Her nightdress was so thin and it clung to her so with the wet that the shape of her breasts and her thighs could be clearly seen. Her short hair was in wringing curls all over her head, and down the lower side of her cheek and jaw sprang a little growth of darkness, as on a youth's still virgin face.

"Come in, now, do," said Olive at the window, and it was as if an evil, black-eyed man were sitting there on the roof, looking distrustingly at the blond young girl in her nightdress as she leaned out into the rain. "You have no right to do like that!" Olive cried out. "If you catch your death, who is it has to nurse you through? You don't think of anyone. I'm cold here, I'm catching cold."

"I'm not cold," said Mildred, and the animal-dark, animal-wounded eyes looked at Olive, and she drew her knees up closer. The shaking of her flesh could be seen, her quivering, dark-haired arms, and the shaking shape of her rain-wet thighs.

"I'm going to call everyone, then," Olive said, hugging herself in her arms for warmth. "I'm going to fetch Dr. Peabody over."

Mildred put her head down on her arms again and she did not answer, and Olive went running downstairs in the little old house. The kitchen was warm, with the fire already red in the kitchener, and Olive ran in and stood shaking in her nightgown with her bare feet on the linoleum floor. The father was eating his breakfast in the kitchen, and the mother was filling the teapot with water from the kettle on the stove.

"Mildred's out on the roof again," she said, rubbing her bare arm in the palms of her hands. Her face was wet from the rain and there were drops of it clinging still in her light, uncombed hair.

"For heaven's sake," said the mother, putting the kettle down, and the two of them ran upstairs after Olive: the mother shaking her short, little hands from her wrists, and the father with egg on his mustaches.

"Come in now, Mildred, do," said the father, standing at the window and looking at his daughter sitting there in the rain. "Come in to us, now, there's a good girl," he said. His hair was gray, but in his mustaches there was still a shade of russet left, like the flesh of a fox's tail. He had not put on his collar yet, and there was a brassy collar button holding his striped shirt together at the neck. His eyes, pale and innocently blue, were wide open on his daughter.

"Come in now to your dad," said the mother with her full neck shaking. "Mildred, lovey, this is no way to do."

"I'm going to fetch Dr. Peabody over," Olive shouted out impatiently at the window, but Mildred did not lift her head. Olive put on her stockings, pulling them up over her plump, hairless legs and twisting them savagely above her knees. Downstairs, she put on her Wellingtons and her raincoat and ran down the path to the gate. Every house in the block was the same, and the same little pieces of garden ran from the front doors to identical gates on the narrow, quiet street. Dr. Peabody's house was on the other side, set apart in the grounds, with trees around it. He did not lose a moment, and in spite of his sixty years he hurried as fast as Olive across the street and into the house where Mildred was sitting on the roof overlooking the back yards.

"Now, Mildred," he said, standing among the members of the family at the window, "I know you want to please us, Mildred. I know you want to be a good girl, don't you? So you're going to make us all happy, and you're going to come in out of the rain."

Mildred looked up at the sound of his voice, her head quickly lifted and a little cocked to one side, as a dog might at the sound of a whistle he knew. But still she had no intention of coming to them.

"I like it here, Dr. Peabody," she said with the rain falling over her face. Her neck was strong and short, like a man's, and broad, with the Adam's apple riding thick and slow in it as she spoke. "I'm not cold, whatever you say. Like this I don't get time to think about other things. I feel hot when I'm lying in bed. I don't feel sick out here in the air like I do closed up in a room, Dr. Peabody."

Dr. Peabody, Dr. Peabody, save me, said the eyes in the thwarted, manlike face. *Let there be some words for the fire in me, that it be suffocated, that it expire. Dr. Peabody, Dr. Peabody,* asked the black, mistrusting eyes, and Dr. Peabody answered:

"Look at your mother and father here, Mildred, look how you're worrying them. Why don't you make up your mind you're not going to act like this any more? Think how happy they'd be if you didn't act like this, Mildred. They've got everything they need to make for happiness in this life, and so have you. Health, and work, and a nice home to live in." Dr. Peabody stood at the window, leaning his old hands on the sill and talking in his equable voice of these things to her: of health and happiness, of tranquillity and love, as if the sound of these words of the sane would draw her back from the brink of where she was. "Come back, Mildred," he said. "You're freezing to death out there, my dear. You mustn't try to make us think you're not. You mustn't try to deceive us, you know. Now, be a good girl and come along in."

"I'm not trying to deceive you, Dr. Peabody," said Mildred, with her black hard, animal eye on him in distrust. "I'm not trying to deceive anybody. Only I don't think I'm a girl. I think something's happening to me. I don't think I'm a girl any more."

"Of course, you're a girl," said Dr. Peabody. He looked at the mother's and father's faces and smiled in gentle sympathy as he quietly shook his head. "Enough of this now, Mildred," he said in a brisker tone. "You come right in now and we'll get you warm and dry, and I'll give you a warm drink that'll send you off to sleep for a little while."

"No," said Mildred, putting her head down again on her bare shaking arms. "I want to stay here."

It was as well the time of year for the birds to be flying, and there was a great movement of them now through the rain. There were small black birds of one kind or another passing over the roofs with quick, unswooping strokes of the wing, and these came, as if in curiosity, to settle on the wires that stretched through the back gardens, and now at the windows of the houses behind there were other onlookers gathering. The family could see the shirt sleeves and the aprons of their neighbors moving with guilt behind the curtains of their kitchen or back bedroom windows, watching the sight of Mildred, wearing nothing but a nightgown, sitting on the roof in the rain.

In a little while, the father had to go off to work, and Dr. Peabody left the house to telephone the police station and tell the constables to come. The last time it had been the fire department that came when Mildred set fire to the rug in the dining room. The mother stayed at the window, talking in a low, loving, tremulous voice to her daughter, but Mildred never answered.

"Leave her be, why don't you?" said Olive in anger as she dressed quickly in the bedroom before the constables would come. She put her corsets on over her soft, white, apple flesh, and snapped her stockings fast. "She's just doing it on purpose," she said over her bare shoulder to her mother. She could not bear to think of the neighbors watching the scene on the roof from their houses. "She ought to be ashamed," she said. She was wondering which of the constables would be sent. She combed her hair out quickly and rolled it into a bun at the back of her neck, and then she put on her brown wool dress. Her face was round and sweet-looking in the glass before her, and she put on her brooch with care. "She ought to be ashamed," she said to her mother bitterly, "sitting there showing her legs and everything like that." She looked a good, pure, healthy girl standing there fixing her hair before the mirror, with her backside shaped out broad and soft in her dress.

The mother turned back from the window and looked at Olive with her little eyes.

"I read a thing in the paper last night," she said, and

she clasped her swollen little hands together. "Maybe it would bring her to her senses, Olive. You run and get me the paper. I don't know what to do."

She had a blue apron tied around her, and her spectacles were on her nose, and when Olive brought her the paper from the kitchen, she stood pressing herself against the sill of the open window, reading the poem out loud to Mildred on the roof.

"Listen to this, Mildred," she said. "You listen, lovely, to what it says. It goes: 'Your body is a jewel box, Given to you to hold A gift that is more precious Than rubies, pearl, or gold.' That's pretty, isn't it, now, Mildred?" Olive stood with her back to the window, angrily fastening on her low, brown shoes. " 'Guard it from marauders,' " the mother's voice went on, reading out loud, " 'Let nothing sordid soil it. No smirch of soot or coal. Your body is a jewel box,' " said the mother's shaking voice, and she could see the neighbors watching slyly from their windows. " 'The jewel is your soul.' "

The mother put down the paper, and there were tears standing underneath her spectacles. She said:

"That means you oughtn't to let all those strange people look at you, Mildred, lovey. You ought to be too proud to let them see you haven't got anything on."

The breath was coming short in her breast, and suddenly the constable's head moved up beyond the rain gutter. There were his helmet and his face just above the rain gutter, and then the tops of his shoulders in his waterproof could be seen. He was standing on a ladder, waiting to be told what to do. Dr. Peabody and another constable came up the stairs without ringing the doorbell and came into the bedroom. Olive saw it was the young constable, and she looked swiftly at her reflection in the glass.

"Mildred," said Dr. Peabody from the window, but Mildred gave no sign. "I've called some friends of mine here to persuade you to come in and put some clothes on. But I know you're going to come along without making any more fuss about it."

But in a little while there was nothing for the young constable to do but to squeeze himself through the window and start making his way across the roof in the rain to where Mildred was sitting.

"If she makes a jump for the edge, you get her," he called out to the other constable, who was waiting on the ladder. He was holding on to the rain pipe now and he nodded his head. The young constable slid cautiously along toward the seated girl, and as he came close to this dark, strange, inhuman creature, a rush of excitement filled his heart. He could see everything clearly through her thin white nightdress, and even the color of her flesh where the cloth clung fast.

All the neighbors were watching from their back windows quite openly now, and some of them were laughing as the constable moved along the sloping roof until he had come between Mildred and the edge. There was just place for him there to squat down, with his hands holding on to the rain-wet shingles.

"Come on, now, Miss," he said, squatting before her in his raincoat. "You must be cold sitting there like that. You don't want to do a thing like that, you know."

Mildred sat with her face hidden in her arms and the rain falling thick and fast upon her, and in every line of her body, in the naked, dark-haired arms, and the shape of the legs revealed, there was a terrible power that roused and impelled him. And yet he felt that he would be sick if he had to touch her with his hands.

"Just help her up here to the window, Constable, please," said Dr. Peabody, leaning out in the rain. The young constable stood up and moved forward toward Mildred, and put his fingers, a little hesitant, underneath her arm. The skin was cold and wet, and he felt his soul recoil within him, and yet she seemed to him a marvelously strange, marvelously evil thing.

"Come along, now, Miss," he urged with a husky voice, and without a word Mildred rose and went with him back up the roof and in through the open window. She stood in the middle of the bedroom, and *Dr. Peabody,* was her anguish saying, *Dr. Peabody, save me from the down springing up on my face and the heaviness in my groins that I cannot give away.* There was no sign of it in her wary eyes as she stood with the rain dripping from her, looking in distrust from one face to the other, looking at her own mother and at her sister and at the doctor and the constable, as if she could never comprehend them as long as she lived.

II

The rain had drawn off for a little in the afternoon, but Olive and Mildred were wearing their raincoats when they left the house. The doctor's double-seated car was stopped by the curb, with the light-tan top up over it and the isinglass curtains fastened all around, and because the doctor could not get off that afternoon, his nephew was sitting in the driver's seat. Beside him sat his friend, the chemist's son, a responsible young man, whom the doctor had asked to go. As the girls came down the front walk to the little gate, the young constable, wearing plain clothes now, got out from the back seat and opened the door of the car for them.

"Mildred's very glad to be going for a ride this afternoon," said Olive, looking the young constable full in the face. The color ran up from under his collar and into his ears as he helped Olive in. The two young men in the front seat of the car lifted their hats and said good afternoon to her. "We've been telling Mildred how nice it was of you to ask us driving," she said, and she gave a sly, quick glance out the open door to the sight of Mildred standing there with her head averted.

"I don't want to go," said Mildred, scarcely aloud.

"Of course, you want to come," said Olive, and she leaned forward and smiled wisely at the young men. "We're just going for a little ride, Mildred. You know that's all we're going to do."

"You help Mildred in, now, Fogarty," said the doctor's nephew, nodding to the constable. The mother was standing in the sitting-room bay, watching them, with her handkerchief up to the side of her face. She saw the young constable help Mildred in, and then follow her into the car, and close the door behind them. When the car started down the street, she waved her handkerchief and the tears fell down her face, but no one in the doctor's car looked out through the yellowing, misted glass.

"I don't want to go," said Mildred. She had a white felt hat on, and her hair stood out dark and bushy from underneath the brim. Her nose was small and pinched in her face and her cheeks were as white as candles. She was holding her bare hands clenched between her legs.

"You're fine and dandy here now, Mildred," said Olive, looking across her to the young constable in his plain brown suit sitting on the other side. "You know it was nice of these young men to ask us out, now, wasn't it, Mildred?" she said, and her mild, blue, wide-set eyes were on the constable.

"I know where you're taking me," said Mildred. The car took the corner of the street and set out fast on the highway.

"We're taking you for a little drive, Mildred," said the doctor's nephew, looking around from the wheel. "You ought to be tickled to death," he said.

He winked at Olive, and she gave him a broad, quick smile.

"All you have to do is to lean back and stop worrying," said the chemist's son.

"I don't want to go there," said Mildred. She was riding with her hands pressed down between her legs and her eyes fixed on the soiled, worn bit of carpet on the floor. The constable had folded his arms across his chest and he rode with his face turned away from Mildred, his eyes staring straight at the dark isinglass through which nothing could be seen. The air was beginning to fill with the smell of the girls' rubber coats as the five of them rode in the curtained-in, swaying car.

"Everything's going to be all right, you'll just see," said Olive. She looked, half smiling with pleasure, at the two heads and the shoulders of the young men riding before them, and then she glanced at the constable sitting on the other side. "Mildred's being a very good girl, isn't she, Mr. Fogarty?" she said.

"Yes," said the young constable with a start, and then his voice stopped in his throat.

"I don't want to go there," said Mildred, and he could feel her flesh beside him. Their thighs were pressed close in the unwieldy, shaking car, their knees withdrawn, their feet apart, and he sat looking into the strange afternoon of yellow isinglass, his heart stirred by the wild power of her hidden flesh. It might have been the most beautiful woman of all riding there beside him, for the terrible, the unbearable love he had for her as he looked into the isinglass. But when his gaze slid sideways to her face, he saw there was nothing of beauty about her, but only her youth, and something like perversion in her body or mind, and this appetite that was starving in her, and crying for food whenever he turned away.

"We're not taking you anywhere, Mildred," said the doctor's nephew, looking around from the wheel again and smiling at Olive. "You just trust us and there won't be any trouble."

"I think Mildred ought to be very grateful to you for taking the afternoon off like this, Mr. Fogarty," said Olive, looking across her sister to the young constable. Suddenly Mildred turned her head and looked straight at her sister with her small, black, wary eyes.

"Don't take me there, don't take me there," she said quickly. Her two hands were held down tight between her knees. "Don't do it. Don't do it to me," she said. "Don't do it, Olive."

"Come on now, Mildred," said the chemist's son. He turned halfway around in his seat and looked at Mildred. "Look here, we're all good friends of yours," he said. "You know me, and Kingdom and Jim Fogarty riding there beside you. We wouldn't do anything to do you any harm."

"Don't take me there," said Mildred in a low, quick voice. She looked with her small, inhuman eyes at the chemist's son, at the back of the other man at the wheel, and then she turned to the constable, who sat with his arms folded over beside her. "Please don't take me there," she said.

The road was running now along the edge of the lake, and through the glass of the windshield they could see the quiet waters, wide and black and still, as the deep waters of the sea might be. The constable could not bring himself to look into her face, and he sat watching the toes of his shoes on the carpet near the long, black-strapped shoes of the girl who rode beside him in the car. She was so near to him that he thought his heart would burst with his desire, but then when his gaze slid to the side of her face, he saw there was nothing in it to draw a man: there was nothing in the pinched, white nostril, and in the piece of the hard, thick, manlike neck that showed.

They had been an hour driving, and the doctor's nephew turned around from the wheel and nodded wisely at Olive.

"It won't be much longer now," he said.

At the sound of his voice, Mildred started up as if from sleep and her thigh in the raincoat pressed hard against the constable's leg.

"I don't want to go there," she said, and Olive, with her hands folded over in her lap, smiled at the chemist's son.

"Let's have a song," she said. She looked toward the

constable. "I'm sure you have a good singing voice, Mr. Fogarty," she said.

"I never sing, I can't sing," said the constable, and the color ran into his neck.

"Oh, I'm sure you're a fine singer, Mr. Fogarty," said Olive, smiling. "I always think a good song makes the time pass quicker, don't you?"

"Well, anyone can sing *Tipperary* or anything like that," said the chemist's son. They had finished the stretch of country now and were coming into a town.

"Here's Sloughcombe," said the doctor's nephew, and Mildred said:

"Don't do it. Don't do it to me, Olive."

The darkness was beginning to come, and here and there along the city street a few of the windows were lighted.

"Getting ready for Christmas," said the doctor's nephew above the sound of the car rattling over the cobbles. There were festoons of green and red paper, and strings of tinsel, strung across a stationer's and a toyshop's glass. In a moment they were out of the town and mounting the hill on the other side, and Mildred said:

"Please don't do this to me."

Her voice came out of the dark to them, small and cold, without entreaty or despair. The doctor's nephew leaned forward and turned on the headlights of the car, and on one side of the road the hedges stood up, as green as if flooded with sunlight.

"We're coming to it now," said the chemist's son under his breath, and the doctor's nephew slowed down the car to take the curve at the gateway. As they drove up the private road of the grounds, they could see the lighted windows of a building hidden in the darkness and trees before them, and Olive took a pair of gloves out of her raincoat pocket and drew them over her hands.

"Put your hat on straight," she said quickly to Mildred.

The car came to a stop at the steps of the building. There were bars at the windows, and an attendant in a white coat opened the door to let them in.

III

It was seven o'clock at night by the time they had settled everything for Mildred. They left her sitting on a chair in the big hall, and they went out and got in the car again and drove away.

"Well, it all went off without any trouble, after all," said the doctor's nephew at the wheel.

"She was meek as a lamb, wasn't she?" said Olive. She was sitting in the back seat alone with the constable now. He sat far from her, in the other corner, and she could just make out the shape of him, sitting erect, with his arms folded over, swaying with the motion of the car.

"We ought to be thankful it passed off the way it did," said the chemist's son. "The time I went there with Weston's brother, it took four of us to hold him down. You never knew what he was going to do next. But that was shell shock. That wasn't the same thing."

"You ought to be glad she's where she's off your hands," said the doctor's nephew, driving. "She'll be better off there than anywhere else. When they're like that, it's all the same to them. They don't know if they're home or where they are. They're living on another plane, you know." He said this easily and with authority, for he was studying to be a doctor himself. "You only have to look at her eyes to know she's not like everybody else," he said, watching the road before him. "There's no use trying to reason with them when they're that way."

The lights of the town were coming up before them, and just within the paved street the chemist's son said:

"Why don't we stop and have a drink?"

"That's just what I need," said the doctor's nephew.

Olive glanced at the constable as the car drew up at the curb before the public house. She could see his profile outlined clearly against the dim, glowing curtain of isinglass. His nose was short, like an Irishman's nose, and his lip was long, and his under-jaw was square and firm. Under his brows there was a fringe, and this was the curving brush of his lashes thrusting thick and ferny against the yellow light.

"Come in and have a drink, Olive," said the chemist's son, opening the door of the car. But Olive shook her head.

"I'll wait here," she said, smiling at them. The young constable made no move to get out of the car.

"You drink, Fogarty?" asked the doctor's nephew.

"No," said the constable, shifting a little. "I don't care about having a drink."

"Don't you think you ought to have one after a ride like this?" said Olive, looking toward his corner.

"No, thank you," said the constable, uneasily. Olive watched the other two go through the door to the public bar.

"I thought the weather was going to clear," said Olive,

turning her head again toward Fogarty. "The radio said last night it was going to clear."

"It looks as if it might rain now," said the constable, looking into the isinglass. He cleared his throat, and recrossed his legs. Olive smoothed the front of her raincoat out.

"Well, it passed off very well, didn't it?" she said in a moment.

"Yes," said the constable, starting as he spoke.

"It was the first time I was ever inside an asylum," said Olive, looking toward him brightly. "I suppose it was the first time you were ever inside an asylum, Mr. Fogarty? I think it was a very interesting experience to have."

The two young men came out of the public house and climbed into the car again.

"It certainly sets you up to have a drink like that," said the doctor's nephew. "Fogarty, you and Olive would feel better if you had. We've a long way to go and we won't get home till late."

"You see, I don't like going in," said Fogarty.

"Oh, you're all right without your uniform, aren't you?" said the chemist's son. "Look," he said as the motor started, "I'll run in and get you each a drink. What'll it be, Fogarty?" He opened the front door of the car again and jumped down into the street. "I don't mind having another myself," he said. "What'll it be, Olive?"

"Oh, I'll just have a little whisky," said Olive, "with a splash of soda in it."

"I'll have the same thing," said the constable from the corner of the car.

"Nobody's going to get ahead of me," said the doctor's nephew. He turned the motor off and followed the other man into the bar. Olive and Fogarty sat waiting for their drinks to come.

"They're a pair, the two of them!" said Olive, laughing. But the constable was thinking that if he were a man with a wife there would not be this fear and trembling in him. He was scared of his life that Olive would sit nearer to him, or that she would reach out and touch him with her hand. "I feel as if a weight had been lifted off me," Olive was saying. "We've been talking for months now about taking Mildred to the asylum, and Dr. Peabody has been urging us to do it. Of course, Mom and the rest of us were against it all the time. But I know it's all for the best, and she'll be in good hands there."

The constable sat erect in the corner of the car, with his arms folded over, not daring to turn his head to her, to speak, not daring to see her, for fear that she stir him as Mildred has done. But even as he took down his drink, and the car started off, even then he could feel her turned toward him in the dark. He could see her face, wide and peach-colored under her felt hat, the yellow hair rolled up from her neck in back, and her lips half open.

"I'm sure we've done the right thing for Mildred," she was saying, and the doctor's nephew looked back from the wheel and said:

"Oh, you don't have to worry about that." He talked with authority to her over his shoulder. "They've got good men there," he said. "The kind of methods they put into operation ought to bring anyone around if there's any hope for them. I wouldn't be surprised to see Mildred walk out of there as sane as you and me at the end of a couple of years."

"I know," said Olive, looking toward the constable in the dark.

"Look, there's a pub along here in a minute," said the chemist's son. "What do you say we all pop in and have a drink?"

"That's a good idea," said the doctor's nephew.

This time the four of them went in, and the constable stood a little apart from the others, tall and clean-looking in his plain brown suit, drinking his whisky quickly down. They had two drinks each, and Olive stood at the bar, laughing, with the two young men. The constable saw her pure-white throat, laughing and bare in the collar of her coat, and the color that was shining on her face. He watched the chemist's son put his arm around her as they went out the door. When they got to the car, he said:

"Say, I'm going to join you two in back, Olive. I think you need a chaperon."

"Ha, ha, ha," laughed Olive, getting into the car, as she sat down, gasping with laughter, between Fogarty and the chemist's son. As the doctor's nephew took his place at the wheel and started the motor she began singing: *I'm in the Mood for Love.*

"It's a shame I've got to drive this car," said the doctor's nephew, looking around at her. The chemist's son put his arm around her again.

"You watch the road, Kingdom!" he called out. "You've got enough to keep you busy driving in this rain."

Fogarty could feel Olive's body close to him on the seat. He could feel the pressing of her heavy thigh in the raincoat beside him, and the seeking of her legs for his while she lay in the other man's arms. She was trying to sing, with her head pulled away from the other man in the corner, and he could feel her eyes, and her legs, and her body turning toward him and seeking him out.

But, as if riding in the car with them, there was Mildred as well: the figure bowed double in the raincoat, the hat that was not white any longer, and the voice saying, the voice repeating. He could see the side of the nostril, the down dark on the jawbone, and the man-like neck descending, bone by bone, to where the small breasts sprang. In a moment, he saw that they had stopped again, and the light from another public house was blurring the yellow isinglass.

"Get us a drink, you, Fogarty," said the chemist's son. "I'm not moving from where I am."

"Come along in with me, Fogarty," said the doctor's nephew. "We'll bring those two their drinks outside."

The constable walked into the bar behind Kingdom and began drinking very fast. He drank three whiskies, and then he carried the two glasses out to Olive and the man in the car. He stood on the sidewalk, waiting while they drank, not looking in at them, but lifting his face like a blind man to the fine, fast-falling rain. Kingdom was still drinking when he went back into the bar with the empty glasses, and Fogarty had another glass with him. When he climbed into the back seat of the car again he was thinking of Mildred and how they had left her sitting in the insane-asylum hall.

"Don't, don't, please, don't," came Olive's voice out of the darkness.

"Some chaps have all the luck," said Kingdom from the front seat, jerking his head toward the chemist's son. "You better come up for air, Geoffrey," he said as he started the motor.

"Mind your own business, Kingdom," said the chemist's son in a muffled, tight voice from the depths of the seat of the car.

"I'll call a policeman if you try anything like that," said Olive, laughing. She drew away from him and closer to Fogarty.

"Come on, now, come on," wooed the chemist's son. He was trying to draw her down again into the darkness of the seat. "Come on, come on, now," came his soft whispering, wooing voice as the car went rattling, racing on through the dark and the falling rain.

Fogarty sat upright in the corner, holding his hands fast under his folded arms. Olive's legs were feeling for his, softly, yearningly closing on his as she pulled away from Geoffrey. And if he had a wife, Fogarty was thinking, if he had a wife of his own the fire would not be burning like this in his body. Deeper and deeper, and wilder and wilder burned his blood until he felt that his bones themselves were utterly burned away.

"Say, you chaps back there," said the doctor's nephew with a whine, "you've got all the luck. Who wants to drive this car and let me have a chance?"

"Come on back," Olive called out. "There's always room for one more!"

Suddenly she turned around on the seat and faced the constable in the corner. His leg was running to wax against her, and he could hear the breath in her mouth. The whisky, or madness, or love was swinging in his head as he put his arms in agony around her, and her mouth came wet and moaning to his mouth.

"Hey, Fogarty—" shouted the chemist's son, and Kingdom looked back, whining, from the wheel.

"Say, I've been among the onlookers just about long—" he began, but he did not finish. What they took for a sudden downpouring of the rain hit the glass of the windshield like a wave, and the lights went out with it, without terror, and without sound. The movement of the car had ceased as if a hand had closed upon it in the dark.

It was not until the next afternoon that anyone thought of looking into the lake for the doctor's car, and there it was, sure enough, with the marks showing clearly where it had left the road. The four corpses were sitting in it, the four young people, just as death had found them, inside the curtains of isinglass.

TILLIE OLSEN

O Yes

I

They are the only white people there, sitting in the dimness of the Negro church that had once been a corner store, and all through the bubbling, swelling, seething of before the services, twelve-year-old Carol clenches tight her mother's hand, the other resting lightly on her friend, Parialee Phillips, for whose baptism she has come.

The white-gloved ushers hurry up and down the aisle, beckoning people to their seats. A jostle of people. To the chairs angled to the left for the youth choir, to the chairs angled to the right for the ladies' choir, even up to the platform, where behind the place for the dignitaries and the mixed choir, the new baptismal tank gleams—and as if pouring into it from the ceiling, the blue-painted River of Jordan, God standing in the waters, embracing a brown man in a leopard skin and pointing to the letters of gold:

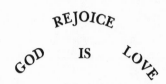

REJOICE

GOD IS LOVE

I AM THE WAY   THE TRUTH   THE LIFE

At the clear window, the crucified Christ embroidered on the starched white curtain leaps in the wind of the sudden singing. And the choirs march in. Robes of wine, of blue, of red.

"We stands and sings too," says Parialee's mother, Alva, to Helen; though already Parialee has pulled Carol up. Singing, little Lucinda Phillips fluffs out her many petticoats; singing, little Bubbie bounces up and down on his heels.

> *Any day now I'll reach that land of freedom,*
> *Yes, o yes*
> *Any day now, know that promised land*

The youth choir claps and taps to accent the swing of it. Beginning to tap, Carol stiffens. "Parry, look. Somebody from school."

"Once more once," says Parialee, in the new way she likes to talk now.

"Eddie Garlin's up there. He's in my math."

"Couple cats from Franklin Jr. chirps in the choir. No harm or alarm."

Anxiously Carol scans the faces to see who else she might know, who else might know her, but looks quickly down to Lucinda's wide skirts, for it seems Eddie looks back at her, sullen or troubled, though it is hard to tell, faced as she is into the window of curtained sunblaze.

> *I know my robe will fit me well*
> *I tried it on at the gates of hell*

If it were a record she would play it over and over, Carol thought, to untwine the intertwined voices, to search how the many rhythms rock apart and yet are one glad rhythm.

> *When I get to heaven gonna sing and shout*
> *Nobody be able to turn me out*

"That's Mr. Chairback Evans going to invocate," Lucinda leans across Parry to explain. "He don't invoke good like Momma."

"Shhhh."

"Momma's the only lady in the church that invocates. She made the prayer last week. (Last month, Lucy.) I made the children's 'nouncement last time. (That was way back Thanksgiving.) And Bubbie's 'nounced too. Lots of times."

"Lucy-inda. SIT!"

Bible study announcements and mixed-choir practice announcements and Teen Age Hearts meeting announcements.

If Eddie said something to her about being there, worried Carol, if he talked to her right in front of somebody
at school.

Messengers of Faith announcements and Mamboettes
announcement and Committee for the Musical Tea.

Parry's arm so warm. Not realizing, starting up the old
game from grade school, drumming a rhythm on the other's
arm to see if the song could be guessed. "Parry, guess."

But Parry is pondering the platform.

The baptismal tank? "Parry, are you scared . . . the bap-
tizing?"

"This cat? No." Shaking her head so slow and scornful,
the barrette in her hair, sun fired, strikes a long rail of
light. And still ponders the platform.

New Strangers Baptist Church invites you and Canaan
Fair Singers announcements and Battle of Song and Cos-
mopolites meet. "O Lord, I couldn't find no ease," a solo.
The ladies' choir:

> *O what you say seekers, o what you say seekers,*
> *Will you never turn back no more?*

The mixed choir sings:

> *Ezekiel saw that wheel of time*
> *Every spoke was of humankind . . .*

And the slim worn man in the pin-stripe suit starts his
sermon On the Nature of God. How God is long-suffering.
Oh, how long he has suffered. Calling the roll of the mighty
nations, that rose and fell and now are dust for grinding
the face of Man.

Voice of drowsiness and dream to which Carol does not need to listen. As long ago. Parry warm beside her too, as it used to be, there in the classroom at Mann Elementary, and the feel of drenched in sun and dimness and dream. Smell and sound of the chalk wearing itself away to nothing, rustle of books, drumming tattoo of fingers on her arm: *Guess.*

And as the preacher's voice spins happy and free, it is the used-to-be play-yard. Tag. Thump of the volley ball. Ecstasy of the jump rope. Parry, do pepper. Carol, do pepper. Parry's bettern Carol, Carol's bettern Parry....

Did someone scream?

It seemed someone screamed—but all were sitting as before, though the sun no longer blared through the windows. She tried to see up where Eddie was, but the ushers were standing at the head of the aisle now, the ladies in white dresses like nurses or waitresses wear, the men holding their white-gloved hands up so one could see their palms.

"And God is Powerful," the preacher was chanting. "Nothing for him to scoop out the oceans and pat up the mountains. Nothing for him to scoop up the miry clay and create man. Man, I said, create Man."

The lady in front of her moaned *"O yes"* and others were moaning *"O yes."*

"And when the earth mourned the Lord said, Weep not, for all will be returned to you, every dust, every atom. And the tired dust settles back, goes back. Until that Judgment Day. That great day."

"O yes."

The ushers were giving out fans. Carol reached for one

and Parry said: What *you* need one for?" but she took it anyway.

"You think Satchmo can blow; you think Muggsy can blow; you think Dizzy can blow?" He was straining to an imaginary trumpet now, his head far back and his voice coming out like a trumpet.

"Oh Parry, he's so good."

"Well. Jelly jelly."

"Nothing to Gabriel on that great getting-up morning. And the horn wakes up Adam and, Adam runs to wake up Eve, and Eve moans; Just one more minute, let me sleep, and Adam yells, Great Day, woman, don't you know it's the Great Day?"

"Great Day, Great Day," the mixed choir behind the preacher rejoices:

> *When our cares are past*
> *when we're home at last ...*

"And Eve runs to wake up Cain." Running round the platform, stooping and shaking imaginary sleepers, "and Cain runs to wake up Abel." Looping, scalloping his voice—"Grea-aaa-aat Daaaay." All the choirs thundering:

> *Great Day*
> *When the battle's fought*
> *And the victory's won*

Exultant spirals of sound. And Carol caught into it (Eddie forgotten, the game forgotten) chanting with Lucy and Bubbie: *"Great Day."*

"Ohhhhhhhhhh," his voice like a trumpet again, "the re-unioning. Ohhhhhhhhh, the rejoicing. After the ages immemorial of longing."

Someone *was* screaming. And an awful thrumming sound with it, like feet and hands thrashing around, like a giant jumping of a rope.

"Great Day." And no one stirred or stared as the ushers brought a little woman out into the aisle, screaming and shaking, just a little shrunk-up woman, not much taller than Carol, the biggest thing about her her swollen hands and the cascades of tears wearing her face.

The shaking inside Carol too. Turning and trembling to ask: "What? . . . that lady?" But Parry still ponders the platform; little Lucy loops the chain of her bracelet round and round; and Bubbie sits placidly, dreamily. Alva Phillips is up fanning a lady in front of her; two lady ushers are fanning other people Carol cannot see. And her mother, her mother looks in a sleep.

Yes. He raised up the dead from the grave. He made old death behave.

Yes. Yes. From all over, hushed. *O Yes*

He was your mother's rock. Your father's mighty tower. And he gave us a little baby. A little baby to love.

I am so glad

Yes, your friend, when you're friendless. Your father when you're fatherless. Way maker. Door opener.

Yes

When it seems you can't go on any longer, he's there. You can, he says, you can.

Yes

And that burden you been carrying—ohhhhh that burden —not for always will it be. No, not for always.

I will put my Word in you and it is power. I will put my Truth in you and it is power.

O Yes

Out of your suffering I will make you to stand as a stone. A tried stone. Hewn out of the mountains of ages eternal.

Yes yes   O Yes

Ohhhhhhhhhh. Out of the mire I will lift your feet. Your tired feet from so much wandering. From so much work and wear and hard times.

Yes

From so much journeying—and never the promised land. And I'll wash them in the well your tears made. And I'll shod them in the gospel of peace, and of feeling good. Ohhhhhhhhh.

Yes.

Behind Carol, a trembling wavering scream. Then the thrashing. Up above, the singing:

They taken my blessed Jesus and flogged him to the woods
And they made him hew out his cross and they dragged
*   him to Calvary*
Shout, brother. Shout shout shout. He never cried a word.

Powerful throbbing voices. Calling and answering to each other.

They taken my blessed Jesus and whipped him up the hill

*With a knotty whip and a raggedy thorn he never cried a
  word*
Shout, sister. Shout shout shout. He never cried a word.

Go tell the people the Saviour has risen
Has risen from the dead and will live forevermore
             And won't have to die no more.
Halleloo.
             Shout, brother, shout
             We won't have to die no more!

A single exultant lunge of shriek. Then the thrashing.
All around a clapping. Shouts with it. The piano whipping, whipping air to a froth. Singing now.

         I once was lost who now am found
         Was blind who now can see

On Carol's fan, a little Jesus walked on wondrously blue
waters to where bearded disciples spread nets out of a fish-
ing boat. If she studied the fan—became it—it might
make a wall around her. If she could make what was happening (*what* was happening?) into a record small and
round to listen to far and far as if into a seashell—the
stamp and rills and spirals all tiny (but never any screaming).

         wade wade in the water

         Jordan's water is chilly and wild
         I've got to get home to the other side
         God's going to trouble the waters

The music leaps and prowls. Ladders of screamings. Drumming feet of ushers running. And still little Lucy fluffs her skirts, loops the chain on her bracelet; still Bubbie sits and rocks dreamily; and only eyes turn for an instant to the aisle as if nothing were happening. "Mother, let's go home," Carol begs, but her mother holds her so tight. Alva Phillips, strong Alva, rocking too and chanting, *O Yes*. No, do not look.

> *Wade,*
> *Sea of trouble all mingled with fire*
> *Come on my brethren it's time to go higher*
> *Wade wade*

The voices in great humming waves, slow, slow (when did it become the humming?), everyone swaying with it too, moving like in slow waves and singing, and up where Eddie is, a new cry, wild and open, "O help me, Jesus," and when Carol opens her eyes she closes them again, quick, but still can see the new known face from school (not Eddie), the thrashing, writhing body, struggling against the ushers with the look of grave and loving support on their faces, and hear the torn, tearing cry: "Don't take me away, life everlasting, don't take me away."

And now the rhinestones in Parry's hair glitter wicked, the white hands of the ushers, fanning, foam in the air; the blue-painted waters of Jordan swell and thunder; Christ spirals on his cross in the window, and she is drowned under the sluice of the slow singing and the sway.

So high up and forgotten the waves and the world, so stirless the deep cool green and the wrecks of what had been. Here now Hostess Foods, where Alva Phillips works her nights—but different from that time Alva had taken them through before work, for it is all sunken under water, the creaking loading platform where they had left the night behind; the closet room where Alva's swaddles of sweaters, boots, and cap hung, the long hall lined with pickle barrels, the sharp freezer door swinging open.

Bubbles of breath that swell. A gulp of numbing air. She swims into the chill room where the huge wheels of cheese stand, and Alva swims too, deftly oiling each machine: slicers and wedgers and the convey, that at her touch start to roll and grind. The light of day blazes up and Alva is holding a cup, saying: Drink this, baby.

"DRINK IT." Her mother's voice and the numbing air demanding her to pay attention. Up through the waters and into the car.

"That's right, lambie, now lie back." Her mother's lap.

"Mother."

"Shhhhh. You almost fainted, lambie."

Alva's voice. "You gonna be all right, Carol . . . Lucy, I'm telling you for the last time, you and Buford get back into that church. Carol is *fine*."

"Lucyinda, if I had all your petticoats I could float." Crying. "Why didn't you let me wear my full skirt with the petticoats, Mother?"

"Shhhhh, lamb." Smoothing her cheek. "Just breathe, take long deep breaths."

". . . How you doing now, you little ol' consolation prize?" It is Parry, but she does not come in the car or reach to Carol through the open window: "No need to cuss and fuss. You going to be sharp as a tack, Jack."

Answering automatically: "And cool as a fool."

Quick, they look at each other.

"Parry, we have to go home now, don't we, Mother? I almost fainted, didn't I, Mother? . . . Parry, I am sorry I got sick and have to miss your baptism."

"Don't feel sorry. I'll feel better you not there to watch. It was our mommas wanted you to be there, not me."

"Parry!" Three voices.

"Maybe I'll come over to play kickball after. If you feeling better. Maybe. Or bring the pogo." Old shared joys in her voice. "Or any little thing."

In just a whisper: "Or any little thing. Parry. Good-bye, Parry."

And why does Alva have to talk now?

"You all right? You breathin' deep like your momma said? Was it too close 'n hot in there? Did something scare you, Carrie?"

Shaking her head to lie, "No."

"I blames myself for not paying attention. You not used to people letting go that way. Lucy and Bubbie, Parialee, they used to it. They been coming since they lap babies."

"Alva, that's all right. Alva, Mrs. Phillips."

"You *was* scared. Carol, it's something to study about. You'll feel better if you understand."

Trying not to listen.

"You not used to hearing what people keeps inside, Carol. You know how music can make you feel things? Glad or sad or like you can't sit still? That was religion music, Carol."

"I have to breathe deep, Mother said."

"Not everybody feels religion the same way. Some it's in their mouth, but some it's like a hope in their blood, their bones. And they singing songs every word that's real to them, Carol, every word out of they own life. And the preaching finding lodgment in their hearts."

The screaming was tuning up in her ears again, high above Alva's patient voice and the waves lapping and fretting.

"Maybe somebody's had a hard week, Carol, and they locked up with it. Maybe a lot of hard weeks bearing down."

"Mother, my head hurts."

"And they're home, Carol, church is home. Maybe the only place they can feel how they feel and maybe let it come out. So they can go on. And it's all right."

"Please, Alva. Mother, tell Alva my head hurts."

"Get Happy, we call it, and most it's a good feeling, Carol. When you got all that locked up inside you."

"Tell her we have to go home. It's all right, Alva. Please, Mother. Say good-bye. Good-bye."

When I was carrying Parry and her father left me, and I fifteen years old, one thousand miles away from home, sin-sick and never really believing, as still I don't believe all, scorning, for what have it done to help, waiting there in the clinic and maybe sleeping, a voice called: Alva, Alva. So mournful and so sweet: Alva. Fear not, I have loved you from the foundation of the universe. And a little small child tugged on my dress. He was carrying a parade stick, on the end of it a star that outshined the sun. Follow me, he said. And the real sun went down and he hidden his stick. How dark it was, how dark. I could feel the darkness with my hands. And when I could see, I screamed. Dump trucks run, dumping bodies in hell, and a convey line run, never ceasing with souls, weary ones having to stamp and shove them along, and the air like fire. Oh I never want to hear such screaming. Then the little child jumped on a motorbike making a path no bigger than my little finger. But first he greased my feet with the hands of my momma when I was a knee baby. They shined like the sun was on them. Eyes he placed all around my head, and as I journeyed upward after him, it seemed I heard a mourning: "Mama Mama you must help carry the world." The rise and fall of nations I saw. And the voice called again Alva Alva, and I flew into a world of light, multitudes singing, Free, free, I am so glad.

2

Helen began to cry, telling her husband about it.

"You and Alva ought to have your heads examined, taking her there cold like that," Len said. "All right, wreck my best handkerchief. Anyway, now that she's had a bath, her Sunday dinner...."

"And been fussed over," seventeen-year-old Jeannie put in.

"She seems good as new. Now *you* forget it, Helen."

"I can't. Something . . . deep happened. If only I or Alva had told her what it would be like. . . . But I didn't realize."

You don't realize a lot of things, Mother, Jeannie said, but not aloud.

"So Alva talked about it after instead of before. Maybe it meant more that way."

"Oh Len, she didn't listen."

"You don't know if she did or not. Or what there was in the experience for her. . . ."

Enough to pull that kid apart two ways even more, Jeannie said, but still not aloud.

"I was so glad she and Parry were going someplace together again. Now that'll be between them too. Len, they really need, miss each other. What happened in a few months? When I think of how close they were, the hours of makebelieve and dressup and playing ball and collecting. . . ."

"Grow up, Mother." Jeannie's voice was harsh. "Parialee's collecting something else now. Like her own crowd. Like jivetalk and rhythmandblues. Like teachers who treat her like a dummy and white kids who treat her like dirt; like boys who think she's really something and chicks who. . . ."

"Jeannie, I know. It hurts."

"Well, maybe it hurts Parry too. Maybe. At least she's got a crowd. Just don't let it hurt Carol though, 'cause there's nothing she can do about it. That's all through, her and Parialee Phillips, put away with their paper dolls."

"No, Jeannie, no."

"It's like Ginger and me. Remember Ginger, my best friend in Horace Mann. But you hardly noticed when it happened to us, did you . . . because she was white? Yes, Ginger, who's got two kids now, who quit school year before last. Parry's never going to finish either. What's she got to do with Carrie any more? They're going different places. Different places, different crowds. And they're sorting. . . ."

"Now wait, Jeannie. Parry's just as bright, just as capable."

"They're in junior high, Mother. Don't you know about junior high? How they sort? And it's all where you're going. Yes and Parry's colored and Carrie's white. And you have to watch everything, what you wear and how you wear it and who you eat lunch with and how much homework you do and how you act to the teacher and what you laugh at. . . . And run with your crowd."

"It's that final?" asked Len. "Don't you think kids like Carol and Parry can show it doesn't *have* to be that way?"

"They can't. They can't. They don't let you."

"No need to shout," he said mildly. "And who do you mean by 'they' and what do you mean by 'sorting'?"

How they sort. A foreboding of comprehension whirled within Helen. What was it Carol had told her of the Welcome Assembly the first day in junior high? The models showing How to Dress and How Not to Dress and half the girls in their loved new clothes watching their counterparts up on the stage—*their* straight skirt, their sweater, their earrings, lipstick, hairdo—"How Not to Dress," "a bad reputation for your school." It was nowhere in Carol's description, yet picturing it now, it seemed to Helen that a mute cry of violated dignity hung in the air. Later there had been a story of going to another Low 7 homeroom on an errand and seeing a teacher trying to wipe the forbidden lipstick off a girl who was fighting back and cursing. Helen could hear Carol's frightened, self-righteous tones: ". . . and I hope they expel her; she's the kind that gives Franklin Jr. a bad rep; she doesn't care about any-thing and always gets into fights." Yet there was nothing in these incidents to touch the heavy comprehension that waited. . . . Homework, the wonderings those times Jean-nie and Carol needed help: "What if there's no one at home to give the help, and the teachers with their two hun-dred and forty kids a day can't or don't or the kids don't ask and they fall hopelessly behind, what then?"—but this too was unrelated. And what had it been that time about Parry? "Mother, Melanie and Sharon won't go if they know Parry's coming." Then of course you'll go with Parry, she's been your friend longer, she had answered, but where was it they were going and what had finally happened? Len, my head hurts, she felt like saying, in Carol's voice in the car, but Len's eyes were grave on Jean-nie who was saying passionately:

"If you think it's so goddam important why do we have to live here where it's for real; why don't we move to Ivy like Betsy (yes, I know, money), where it's the deal to be buddies, in school anyway, three coloured kids and their father's a doctor or judge or something big wheel and one always gets elected President or head song girl or some-thing to prove oh how we're democratic. . . . What do you want of that poor kid anyway? Make up your mind. Stay friends with Parry—but be one of the kids. Sure. Be a brain —but not a square. Rise on up, college prep, but don't get separated. Yes, stay one of the kids but. . . ."

"Jeannie. You're not talking about Carol at all, are you, Jeannie? Say it again. I wasn't listening. I was trying to think."

"She will not say it again," Len said firmly, "you look

about ready to pull a Carol. One a day's our quota. And you, Jeannie, we'd better cool it. Too much to talk about for one session. . . . Here, come to the window and watch the Carol and Parry you're both all worked up about."

In the wind and the shimmering sunset light, half the children of the block are playing down the street. Leaping, bouncing, hallooing, tugging the kites of spring. In the old synchronized understanding, Carol and Parry kick, catch, kick, catch. And now Parry jumps on her pogo stick (the last time), Carol shadowing her, and Bubbie, arching his body in a semicircle of joy, bounding after them, high, higher, higher.

And the months go by and supposedly it is forgotten, except for the now and then when, self-important, Carol will say: I really truly did nearly faint, didn't I, Mother, that time I went to church with Parry?

And now seldom Parry and Carol walk the hill together. Melanie's mother drives by to pick up Carol, and the several times Helen has suggested Parry, too, Carol is quick to explain: "She's already left" or "She isn't ready; she'll make us late."

And after school? Carol is off to club or skating or library or someone's house, and Parry can stay for kickball only on the rare afternoons when she does not have to hurry home where Lucy, Bubbie, and the cousins wait to be cared for, now Alva works the four to twelve-thirty shift.

No more the bending together over the homework. All semester the teachers have been different, and rarely Parry brings her books home, for where is there space or time and what is the sense? And the phone never rings with: what you going to wear tomorrow, are you bringing your lunch, or come on over, let's design some clothes for the Katy Keane comic-book contest. And Parry never drops by with Alva for Saturday snack to or from grocery shopping.

And the months go by and the sorting goes on and seemingly it is over until that morning when Helen must stay home from work, so swollen and feverish is Carol with mumps.

The afternoon before, Parry had come by, skimming up the stairs, spilling books and binders on the bed: Hey frail, lookahere and wail, your momma askin for homework, what she got against YOU? . . . looking quickly once then not looking again and talking fast. . . . Hey, you bloomed. You gonna be your own pumpkin, hallowe'en? Your momma know yet it's mu-umps? And lumps. Momma say: no distress, she'll be by tomorrow morning see do you need anything while your momma's to work. . . . (Singing: *whole lotta shakin goin on.*) All your 'signments is inside; Miss Rockface says the teachers to write 'em cause I mightn't get it right all right.

But did not tell: Does your mother work for Carol's mother? Oh, you're neighbors! Very well, I'll send along a monitor to open Carol's locker but you're only to take these things I'm writing down, nothing else. Now say after me: Miss Campbell is trusting me to be a good responsible girl. And go right to Carol's house. After school. Not stop anywhere on the way. Not lose anything. And only take. What's written on the list.

You really gonna mess with that book stuff? Sign on *mine* says do-not-open-until-eX-mas. . . . That Mrs. Fernandez doll she didn't send nothin, she was the only, says feel better and read a book to report if you feel like and I'm the most for takin care for you; she's my most, wish I could get her but she only teaches 'celerated. . . . Flicking the old read books on the shelf but not opening to mock-declaim as once she used to . . . Vicky, Eddie's g.f. in Rockface office, she's on suspended for sure, yellin to Rockface: you bitchkitty don't you give me no more bad shit. That Vicky she can sure sling-ating-ring it. Staring out the window as if the tree not there in which they had hid out and rocked so often. . . . For sure. (*Keep mo-o-vin.*) Got me a new pink top and lilac skirt. Look sharp with this purple? Cinching in the wide belt as if delighted with what newly swelled above and swelled below. Wear it Saturday night to Sweet's, Modernaires Sounds of Joy, Leroy and Ginny and me goin if Momma'll stay home. IF. (*Shake my baby shake.*) How come old folks still likes to party? Huh? Asking of Rembrandt's weary old face looking from the wall. How come (softly) you long-gone you. Touching her face to his quickly, lightly. NEXT mumps is your buddybud Melanie's turn to tote your stuff. I'm getting the hoovus goovus. Hey you so unneat, don't care what you bed with. Removing the books and binders, ranging them on the dresser one by one, marking lipstick faces—bemused or mocking or amazed—on each paper jacket.

Better. Fluffing out smoothing the quilt with exaggerated energy. Any little thing I can get, cause I gotta blow. Tossing up and catching their year-ago, arm-in-arm graduation picture, replacing it deftly, upside down, into its mirror crevice. Joe. Bring you joy juice or fizz water or kickapoo? Adding a frown line to one bookface. Twanging the paper fishkite, the Japanese windbell overhead, setting the mobile they had once made of painted eggshells and decorated straws to twirling and rocking. And is gone.

She talked to the lipstick faces after, in her fever, tried to stand on her head to match the picture, twirled and twanged with the violent overhead.

Sleeping at last after the disordered night. Having surrounded herself with the furnishings of that world of childhood she no sooner learned to live in comfortably, then had to leave.

The dollhouse stands there to arrange and rearrange; the shell and picture card collections to re-sort and remember; the population of dolls given away to little sister, borrowed back, propped all around to dress and undress and caress.

She has thrown off her nightgown because of the fever, and her just budding breast is exposed where she reaches to hold the floppy plush dog that had been her childhood pillow.

Not for anything would Helen have disturbed her. Except that in the unaccustomedness of a morning at home, in the bruised restlessness after the sleepless night, she clicks on the radio—and the storm of singing whirls into the room:

> *. . . of trouble all mingled with fire*
> *Come on my brethren we've got to go higher*
> *Wade, wade. . . .*

And Carol runs down the stairs, shrieking and shrieking. "Turn it off, Mother, turn it off." Hurling herself at the dial and wrenching it so it comes off in her hand.

"Ohhhhh," choked and convulsive, while Helen tries to hold her, to quiet.

"Mother, why did they sing and scream like that?"

"At Parry's church?"

"Yes." Rocking and strangling the cries. "I hear it all the time." Clinging and beseeching. ". . . What was it, Mother? Why?"

Emotion, Helen thought of explaining, *a characteristic of the religion of all oppressed peoples, yes your very own great-grandparents*—thought of saying. And discarded.

Aren't you now, haven't you had feelings in yourself so strong they had to come out some way? ("what howls restrained by decorum")—thought of saying. And discarded.

Repeat Alva: *hope . . . every word out of their own life. A place to let go. And church is home.* And discarded.

The special history of the Negro people—history?—just you try living what must be lived every day—thought of saying. And discarded.

And said nothing.

And said nothing.

And soothed and held.

"Mother, a lot of the teachers and kids don't like Parry when they don't even know what she's like. Just because. . . ." Rocking again, convulsive and shamed. "And I'm not really her friend any more."

No news. Betrayal and shame. Who betrayed? Whose shame? Brought herself to say aloud: "But may be friends again. As Alva and I are."

The sobbing a whisper. "That girl Vicky who got that way when I fainted, she's in school. She's the one keeps wearing the lipstick and they wipe it off and she's always in trouble and now maybe she's expelled. Mother."

"Yes, lambie."

"She acts so awful outside but I remember how she was in church and whenever I see her now I have to wonder. And hear . . . like I'm her, Mother, like I'm her." Clinging and trembling. "Oh why do I have to feel it happens to me too?

"Mother, I want to forget about it all, and not care—like Melanie. Why can't I forget? Oh why is it like it is and why do I have to care?"

Caressing, quieting.

Thinking: *caring asks doing. It is a long baptism into the seas of humankind, my daughter. Better immersion than to live untouched. . . . Yet how will you sustain?*

Why is it like it is?

Sheltering her daughter close, mourning the illusion of the embrace.

And why do I have to care?

While in her, her own need leapt and plunged for the place of strength that was not—where one could scream or sorrow while all knew and accepted, and gloved and loving hands waited to support and understand.

For Margaret Heaton, who always taught
1956

FLANNERY O'CONNOR

A Temple of the Holy Ghost

All week end the two girls were calling each other Temple One and Temple Two, shaking with laughter and getting so red and hot that they were positively ugly, particularly Joanne who had spots on her face anyway. They came in the brown convent uniforms they had to wear at Mount St. Scholastica but as soon as they opened their suitcases, they took off the uniforms and put on red skirts and loud blouses. They put on lipstick and their Sunday shoes and walked around in the high heels all over the house, always passing the long mirror in the hall slowly to get a look at their legs. None of their ways were lost on the child. If only one of them had come, that one would have played with her, but since there were two of them, she was out of it and watched them suspiciously from a distance.

They were fourteen—two years older than she was—but neither of them was bright, which was why they had been sent to the convent. If they had gone to a regular school, they wouldn't have done anything but think about boys, at the convent the sisters, her mother said, would keep a grip on their necks. The child decided, after observing them for a few hours, that they were practically morons and she was glad to think that they were only second cousins and she couldn't have inherited any of their stupidity. Susan called herself Su-zan. She was very skinny but she had a pretty pointed face and red hair. Joanne had yellow hair that was naturally curly but she talked through her nose and when she laughed, she turned purple in patches. Neither one of them could say an intelligent thing and all their sentences began, "You know this boy I know well one time he . . ."

They were to stay all week end and her mother said she didn't see how she would entertain them since she didn't know any boys their age. At this, the child, struck suddenly with genius, shouted, "There's Cheat! Get Cheat to come! Ask Miss Kirby to get Cheat to come show them around!" and she nearly choked on the food she had in her mouth. She doubled over laughing and hit the table with her fist and looked at the two bewildered girls while water started in her eyes and rolled down her fat cheeks and the braces she had in her mouth glared like tin. She had never thought of anything so funny before.

Her mother laughed in a guarded way and Miss Kirby blushed and carried her fork delicately to her mouth with one pea on it. She was a long-faced blonde schoolteacher who boarded with them and Mr. Cheatam was her admirer, a rich old farmer who arrived every Saturday afternoon in a fifteen-year-old baby-blue Pontiac powdered with red clay dust and black inside with Negroes that he charged ten cents apiece to bring into town on Saturday afternoons. After he dumped them he came to see Miss Kirby, always bringing a little gift—a bag of boiled peanuts or a watermelon or a stalk of sugar cane and once a wholesale box of Baby Ruth candy bars. He was bald-headed except for a little fringe of rust-colored hair and his face was nearly the same color as the unpaved roads and washed like them with ruts and gulleys. He wore a pale green shirt with a thin black stripe in it and blue galluses and his trousers cut across a protruding stomach that he pressed tenderly from time to time with his big flat thumb. All his teeth were backed with gold and he would roll his eyes at Miss Kirby in an impish way and say, "Haw haw," sitting in their porch swing with his legs spread apart and his hightopped shoes pointing in opposite directions on the floor.

"I don't think Cheat is going to be in town this weekend," Miss Kirby said, not in the least understanding that this was a joke, and the child was convulsed afresh, threw herself backward in her chair, fell out of it, rolled on the floor and lay there heaving. Her mother told her if she didn't stop this foolishness she would have to leave the table.

Yesterday her mother had arranged with Alonzo Myers to drive them the forty-five miles to Mayville, where the convent was, to get the girls for the week end and Sunday afternoon he was hired to drive them back again. He was an eighteen-year-old boy who weighed two hundred and fifty pounds and worked for the taxi company and he was all you could get to drive you anywhere. He smoked or rather chewed a short black cigar and he had a round sweaty chest that showed through the yellow nylon shirt he wore. When he drove all the windows of the car had to be open.

"Well there's Alonzo!" the child roared from the floor. "Get Alonzo to show em around! Get Alonzo!"

The two girls, who had seen Alonzo, began to scream their indignation.

Her mother thought this was funny too but she said, "That'll be about enough out of you," and changed the subject. She asked them why they called each other Temple One and Temple Two and this sent them off into gales of giggles. Finally they managed to explain. Sister Perpetua, the oldest nun at the Sisters of Mercy in Mayville, had given them a lecture on what to do if a young man should —here they laughed so hard they were not able to go on without going back to the beginning—on what to do if a young man should—they put their heads in their laps—on what to do if—they finally managed to shout it out—if he should "behave in an ungentlemanly manner with them in the back of an automobile." Sister Perpetua said they were to say, "Stop sir! I am a Temple of the Holy Ghost!" and that would put an end to it. The child sat up off the floor with a blank face. She didn't see anything so funny in this. What was really funny was the idea of Mr. Cheatam or Alonzo Myers beauing them around. That killed her.

Her mother didn't laugh at what they had said. "I think

you girls are pretty silly," she said. "After all, that's what you are—Temples of the Holy Ghost."

The two of them looked up at her, politely concealing their giggles, but with astonished faces as if they were beginning to realize that she was made of the same stuff as Sister Perpetua.

Miss Kirby preserved her set expression and the child thought, it's all over her head anyhow. I am a Temple of the Holy Ghost, she said to herself, and was pleased with the phrase. It made her feel as if somebody had given her a present.

After dinner, her mother collapsed on the bed and said, "Those girls are going to drive me crazy if I don't get some entertainment for them. They're awful."

"I bet I know who you could get," the child started.

"Now listen. I don't want to hear any more about Mr. Cheatam," her mother said. "You embarrass Miss Kirby. He's her only friend. Oh my Lord," and she sat up and looked mournfully out the window, "that poor soul is so lonesome she'll even ride in that car that smells like the last circle in hell."

And she's a Temple of the Holy Ghost too, the child reflected. "I wasn't thinking of him," she said. "I was thinking of those two Wilkinses, Wendell and Cory, that visit old lady Buchell out on her farm. They're her grandsons. They work for her."

"Now that's an idea," her mother murmured and gave her an appreciative look. But then she slumped again. "They're only farm boys. These girls would turn up their noses at them."

"Huh," the child said. "They wear pants. They're sixteen and they got a car. Somebody said they were both going to be Church of God preachers because you don't have to know nothing to be one."

"They would be perfectly safe with those boys all right," her mother said and in a minute she got up and called their grandmother on the telephone and after she had talked to the old woman a half an hour, it was arranged that Wendell and Cory would come to supper and afterwards take the girls to the fair.

Susan and Joanne were so pleased that they washed their hair and rolled it up on aluminum curlers. Hah, thought the child, sitting cross-legged on the bed to watch them undo the curlers, wait'll you get a load of Wendell and Cory! "You'll like these boys," she said. "Wendell is six feet tall ands got red hair. Cory is six feet six inches talls got black hair and wears a sport jacket and they gottem this car with a squirrel tail on the front."

"How does a child like you know so much about these men?" Susan asked and pushed her face up close to the mirror to watch the pupils in her eyes dilate.

The child lay back on the bed and began to count the narrow boards in the ceiling until she lost her place. I know them all right, she said to someone. We fought in the world war together. They were under me and I saved them five times from Japanese suicide divers and Wendell said I am going to marry that kid and the other said oh no you ain't I am and I said neither one of you is because I will court marshall you all before you can bat an eye. "I've seen them around is all," she said.

When they came the girls stared at them a second and then began to giggle and talk to each other about the convent. They sat in the swing together and Wendell and Cory sat on the banisters together. They sat like monkeys, their knees on a level with their shoulders and their arms hanging down between. They were short thin boys with red faces and high cheekbones and pale seed-like eyes. They had brought a harmonica and a guitar. One of them began to blow softly on the mouth organ, watching the girls over it, and the other started strumming the guitar and then began to sing, not watching them but keeping his head tilted upward as if he were only interested in hearing himself. He was singing a hillbilly song that sounded half like a love song and half like a hymn.

The child was standing on a barrel pushed into some bushes at the side of the house, her face on a level with the porch floor. The sun was going down and the sky was turning a bruised violet color that seemed to be connected with the sweet mournful sound of the music. Wendell began to smile as he sang and to look at the girls. He looked at Susan with a dog-like loving look and sang,

> *"I've found a friend in Jesus,*
> *He's everything to me,*
> *He's the lily of the valley,*
> *He's the One who's set me free!"*

Then he turned the same look on Joanne and sang,

> *"A wall of fire about me,*

I've nothing now to fear,
He's the lily of the valley,
And I'll always have Him near!"

The girls looked at each other and held their lips stiff so as not to giggle but Susan let out one anyway and clapped her hand on her mouth. The singer frowned and for a few seconds only strummed the guitar. Then he began "The Old Rugged Cross" and they listened politely but when he had finished they said, "Let us sing one!" and before he could start another, they began to sing with their convent-trained voices,

"Tantum ergo Sacramentum
Veneremur Cernui:
Et antiquum documentum
Novo cedat ritui:"

The child watched the boys' solemn faces turn with perplexed frowning stares at each other as if they were uncertain whether they were being made fun of.

"Praestet fides supplementum
Sensuum defectui.

Genitori, Genitoque
Laus et jubilatio
Salus, honor, virtus quoque . . ."

The boys' faces were dark red in the gray-purple light. They looked fierce and startled.

> *"Sit et benedictio;*
> *Procedenti ab utroque*
> *Compar sit laudatio.*
> *Amen."*

The girls dragged out the Amen and then there was a silence.

"That must be Jew singing," Wendell said and began to tune the guitar.

The girls giggled idiotically but the child stamped her foot on the barrel. "You big dumb ox!" she shouted. "You big dumb Church of God ox!" she roared and fell off the barrel and scrambled up and shot around the corner of the house as they jumped from the banister to see who was shouting.

Her mother had arranged for them to have supper in the back yard and she had a table laid out there under some Japanese lanterns that she pulled out for garden parties. "I ain't eating with them," the child said and snatched her plate off the table and carried it to the kitchen and sat down with the thin blue-gummed cook and ate her supper.

"How come you be so ugly sometime?" the cook asked.

"Those stupid idiots," the child said.

The lanterns gilded the leaves of the trees orange on the level where they hung and above them was black-green and below them were different dim muted colors that made the girls sitting at the table look prettier than they were. From time to time, the child turned her head and glared out the kitchen window at the scene below.

"God could strike you deaf dumb and blind," the cook said, "and then you wouldn't be as smart as you is."

"I would still be smarter than some," the child said.

After supper they left for the fair. She wanted to go to the fair but not with them so even if they had asked her she wouldn't have gone. She went upstairs and paced the long bedroom with her hands locked together behind her back and her head thrust forward and an expression, fierce and dreamy both, on her face. She didn't turn on the electric light but let the darkness collect and make the room smaller and more private. At regular intervals a light crossed the open window and threw shadows on the wall. She stopped and stood looking out over the dark slopes, past where the pond glinted silver, past the wall of woods to the speckled sky where a long finger of light was revolving up and around and away, searching the air as if it were hunting for the lost sun. It was the beacon light from the fair.

She could hear the distant sound of the calliope and she saw in her head all the tents raised up in a kind of gold sawdust light and the diamond ring of the ferris wheel going around and around up in the air and down again and the screeking merry-go-round going around and around on the ground. A fair lasted five or six days and there was a special afternoon for school children and a special night for niggers. She had gone last year on the afternoon for school children and had seen the monkeys and the fat man and had ridden on the ferris wheel. Certain tents were closed then because they contained things that would be known only to grown people but she had looked with interest at the advertising on the closed tents, at the faded-looking pictures on the canvas of people in tights, with stiff stretched composed faces like the faces of the martyrs waiting to have their tongues cut out by the Roman soldier. She had imagined that what was inside these tents concerned medicine and she had made up her mind to be a doctor when she grew up.

She had since changed and decided to be an engineer but as she looked out the window and followed the revolving searchlight as it widened and shortened and wheeled in its arc, she felt that she would have to be much more than just a doctor or an engineer. She would have to be a saint because that was the occupation that included everything you could know; and yet she knew she would never be a saint. She did not steal or murder but she was a born liar and slothful and she sassed her mother and was deliberately ugly to almost everybody. She was eaten up also with the sin of Pride, the worst one. She made fun of the Baptist preacher who came to the school at commencement to give the devotional. She would pull down her mouth and hold her forehead as if she were in agony and groan, "Fawther, we thank Thee," exactly the way he did and she had been told many times not to do it. She could never be a saint, but she thought she could be a martyr if they killed her quick.

She could stand to be shot but not to be burned in oil. She didn't know if she could stand to be torn to pieces by lions or not. She began to prepare her martyrdom, seeing herself in a pair of tights in a great arena, lit by the early Christians hanging in cages of fire, making a gold dusty light that fell on her and the lions. The first lion charged forward and fell at her feet, converted. A whole series of lions did the same. The lions liked her so much she even slept with them and finally the Romans were obliged to burn her but to their astonishment she would not burn down and finding she was so hard to kill, they finally cut off her head very quickly with a sword and she went immediately to heaven. She rehearsed this several times, returning each time at the entrance of Paradise to the lions.

Finally she got up from the window and got ready for bed and got in without saying her prayers. There were two heavy double beds in the room. The girls were occupying the other one and she tried to think of something cold and clammy that she could hide in their bed but her thought was fruitless. She didn't have anything she could think of, like a chicken carcass or a piece of beef liver. The sound of the calliope coming through the window kept her awake and she remembered that she hadn't said her prayers and got up and knelt down and began them. She took a running start and went through to the other side of the Apostles' Creed and then hung by her chin on the side of the bed, empty-minded. Her prayers, when she remembered to say them, were usually perfunctory but sometimes when she had done something wrong or heard music or lost something, or sometimes for no reason at all, she would be moved to fervor and would think of Christ on the long journey to Calvary, crushed three times under the rough cross. Her mind would stay on this a while and then get empty and when something roused her, she would find that she was thinking of a different thing entirely, of some dog or some girl or something she was going to do some day. Tonight, remembering Wendell and Cory, she was filled with thanksgiving and almost weeping with delight, she said, "Lord, Lord, thank You that I'm not in the Church of God, thank You Lord, thank You!" and got back in bed and kept repeating it until she went to sleep.

The girls came in at a quarter to twelve and waked her up with their giggling. They turned on the small blue-shaded lamp to see to get undressed by and their skinny shadows climbed up the wall and broke and continued moving about softly on the ceiling. The child sat up to hear what all they had seen at the fair. Susan had a plastic pistol full of cheap candy and Joanne a pasteboard cat with red polka dots in it. "Did you see the monkeys dance?" the child asked. "Did you see that fat man and those midgets?"

"All kinds of freaks," Joanne said. And then she said to Susan, "I enjoyed it all but the you-know-what," and her face assumed a peculiar expression as if she had bit into something that she didn't know if she liked or not.

The other stood still and shook her head once and nodded slightly at the child. "Little pitchers," she said in a low voice but the child heard it and her heart began to beat very fast.

She got out of her bed and climbed onto the footboard of theirs. They turned off the light and got in but she didn't move. She sat there, looking hard at them until their faces were well defined in the dark. "I'm not as old as you all," she said, "but I'm about a million times smarter."

"There are some things," Susan said, "that a child of

your age doesn't know," and they both began to giggle.

"Go back to your own bed," Joanne said.

The child didn't move. "One time," she said, her voice hollow-sounding in the dark, "I saw this rabbit have rabbits."

There was a silence. Then Susan said, "How?" in an indifferent tone and she knew that she had them. She said she wouldn't tell until they told about the you-know-what. Actually she had never seen a rabbit have rabbits but she forgot this as they began to tell what they had seen in the tent.

It had been a freak with a particular name but they couldn't remember the name. The tent where it was had been divided into two parts by a black curtain, one side for men and one for women. The freak went from one side to the other, talking first to the men and then to the women, but everyone could hear. The stage ran all the way across the front. The girls heard the freak say to the men, "I'm going to show you this and if you laugh, God may strike you the same way." The freak had a country voice, slow and nasal and neither high nor low, just flat. "God made me thisaway and if you laugh He may strike you the same way. This is the way He wanted me to be and I ain't disputing His way. I'm showing you because I got to make the best of it. I expect you to act like ladies and gentlemen. I never done it to myself nor had a thing to do with it but I'm making the best of it. I don't dispute hit." Then there was a long silence on the other side of the tent and finally the freak left the men and came over onto the women's side and said the same thing

The child felt every muscle strained as if she were hearing the answer to a riddle that was more puzzling than the riddle itself. "You mean it had two heads?" she said.

"No," Susan said, "it was a man and woman both. It pulled up its dress and showed us. It had on a blue dress."

The child wanted to ask how it could be a man and woman both without two heads but she did not. She wanted to get back into her own bed and think it out and she began to climb down off the footboard.

"What about the rabbit?" Joanne asked.

The child stopped and only her face appeared over the footboard, abstracted, absent. "It spit them out of its mouth," she said, "six of them."

She lay in bed trying to picture the tent with the freak walking from side to side but she was too sleepy to figure it out. She was better able to see the faces of the country people watching, the men more solemn than they were in church, and the women stern and polite, with painted-looking eyes, standing as if they were waiting for the first note of the piano to begin the hymn. She could hear the freak saying, "God made me thisaway and I don't dispute hit," and the people saying, "Amen. Amen."

"God done this to me and I praise Him."

"Amen. Amen."

"He could strike you thisaway."

"Amen. Amen."

"But He has not."

"Amen."

"Raise yourself up. A temple of the Holy Ghost. You! You are God's temple, don't you know? Don't you know? God's Spirit has a dwelling in you, don't you know?"

"Amen. Amen."

"If anybody desecrates the temple of God, God will bring him to ruin and if you laugh, He may strike you thisaway. A temple of God is a holy thing. Amen. Amen."

"I am a temple of the Holy Ghost."

"Amen."

The people began to slap their hands without making a loud noise and with a regular beat between the Amens, more and more softly, as if they knew there was a child near, half asleep.

The next afternoon the girls put on their brown convent uniforms again and the child and her mother took them back to Mount St. Scholastica. "Oh glory, oh Pete!" they said. "Back to the salt mines." Alonzo Myers drove them and the child sat in front with him and her mother sat in back between the two girls, telling them such things as how pleased she was to have had them and how they must come back again and then about the good times she and their mothers had had when they were girls at the convent. The child didn't listen to any of this twaddle but kept as close to the locked door as she could get and held her head out the window. They had thought Alonzo would smell better on Sunday but he did not. With her hair blowing over her face she could look directly into the ivory sun which was framed in the middle of the blue afternoon but when she pulled it away from her eyes she had to squint.

Mount St. Scholastica was a red brick house set back in a garden in the center of town. There was a filling station on one side of it and a firehouse on the other. It had a high black grillework fence around it and narrow bricked walks between old trees and japonica bushes that were heavy with blooms. A big moon-faced nun came bustling to the door to let them in and embraced her mother and would have done the same to her but that she stuck out her hand and preserved a frigid frown, looking just past the sister's shoes at the wainscoting. They had a tendency to kiss even homely children, but the nun shook her hand vigorously and even cracked her knuckles a little and said they must come to the chapel, that benediction was just beginning. You put your foot in their door and they got you praying, the child thought as they hurried down the polished corridor.

You'd think she had to catch a train, she continued in the same ugly vein as they entered the chapel where the sisters were kneeling on one side and the girls, all in brown uniforms, on the other. The chapel smelled of incense. It was light green and gold, a series of springing arches that ended with the one over the altar where the priest was kneeling in front of the monstrance, bowed low. A small boy in a surplice was standing behind him, swinging the censer. The child knelt down between her mother and the nun and they were well into the *"Tantum Ergo"* before her ugly thoughts stopped and she began to realize that she was in the presence of God. Hep me not to be so mean, she began mechanically. Hep me not to give her so much sass. Hep me not to talk like I do. Her mind began to get quiet and then empty but when the priest raised the monstrance with the Host shining ivory-colored in the center of it, she was thinking of the tent at the fair that had the freak in it. The freak was saying, "I don't dispute hit. This is the way He wanted me to be."

As they were leaving the convent door, the big nun swooped down on her mischievously and nearly smothered her in the black habit, mashing the side of her face into the crucifix hitched onto her belt and then holding her off and looking at her with little periwinkle eyes.

On the way home she and her mother sat in the back and Alonzo drove by himself in the front. The child observed three folds of fat in the back of his neck and noted that his ears were pointed almost like a pig's. Her mother, making conversation, asked him if he had gone to the fair.

"Gone," he said, "and never missed a thing and it was good I gone when I did because they ain't going to have it next week like they said they was."

"Why?" asked her mother.

"They shut it on down," he said. "Some of the preachers from town gone out and inspected it and got the police to shut it on down."

Her mother let the conversation drop and the child's round face was lost in thought. She turned it toward the window and looked out over a stretch of pasture land that rose and fell with a gathering greenness until it touched the dark woods. The sun was a huge red ball like an elevated Host drenched in blood and when it sank out of sight, it left a line in the sky like a red clay road hanging over the trees.

BIOGRAPHICAL NOTES

KAY BOYLE was born in St. Paul, Minnesota, in 1903. After living in France, England, and Austria for several years, she returned to the United States in 1941. After World War II, she moved to Germany, where she acted as European correspondent for the *The New Yorker* magazine. Author of more than twenty books, she is especially noted as a writer of short stories. Some of her collections include *Wedding Day, The First Lover, The White Horses of Vienna, The Crazy Hunter,* and *The Smoking Mountain.* Miss Boyle is now on the faculty of San Francisco State College.

COLETTE was born in 1873 in Burgundy, France. She wrote her first stories in her early twenties at the suggestion of her husband, who later had them published under his name. They were an overwhelming popular success in Paris. After her divorce, Colette took up a career as a dancer and mime in French vaudeville, which she describes with accuracy and humor in *The Vagabond* and *Music Hall Sidelights.* Colette's many novels include *Cheri, The Last of Cheri,* and *Gigi;* her collections of short stories include *The Tender Shoot* and *The Ripening Seed.* Famous for her wit and her considerable descriptive powers, Colette is also known for her uncanny ability to project the essence of the female experience, setting down the lives of her women with candor, sympathy, and precision. She died in 1954.

SHIRLEY ANN GRAU was born in New Orleans in 1929. Her first collection of stories, *The Black Prince,* published when she was twenty-six, won universal praise and established her reputation as one of the finest writers in the American Southern tradition. Since then she has written several novels, including *Keepers of the House* and *The Condor Passes*.

R. PRAWER JHABVALA was born of Polish parents in Germany and came to England with them in 1939, at the age of twelve. She was educated in England and took her degree in English literature at London University. In 1951 she married C. S. H. Jhabvala, an Indian architect, and they and their three daughters now live in Delhi. She has written five novels about India: *Amrita, The Nature of Passion, Esmond in India, The Householder,* and *Get Ready for Battle*.

DORIS LESSING was born in 1919 in Iran, went to school in Southern Rhodesia, and has lived in London since 1949, when she arrived with the manuscript of her first novel, *The Grass Is Singing*. This was published almost immediately and has been reprinted many times. Miss Lessing has written many short stories, several novels, and two successful plays. Perhaps her best-known work is *The Golden Notebook* (1962), one of the most perceptive and revealing books about women in contemporary fiction.

CARSON McCULLERS was born in 1917 in Columbus, Georgia, wrote seriously from the age of sixteen, and studied at Columbia University and New York University. She made her indelible mark on American literature in her early twenties with the publication of *The Heart Is a Lonely Hunter,* one of the classics of modern Southern fiction. Some of her other works include *Reflections in a Golden Eye, The Ballad of the Sad Cafe,* and *Clock Without Hands.* In 1943 she was given an award by the American Academy of Arts and Letters, and in 1950 the play *The Member of the Wedding,* adapted from her novel, won the New York Drama Critics' Circle Award for Best Play of the Year. Mrs. McCullers, who has been ranked with Faulkner and Hemingway by international critics, died in 1967.

EDNA O'BRIEN was born in 1931 in the West of Ireland and now lives in London with her two sons. She has written *The Country Girls, The Girl with the Green Eyes, Girls in Their Married Bliss, August Is a Wicked Month, Casualties of Peace, The Love Object, A Pagan Place,* and *X, Y & Zee.*

FLANNERY O'CONNOR was born in Savannah, Georgia, in 1925. She graduated from Georgia State College for Women and studied creative writing at the State University of Iowa. Her first short story was published in 1946, but it was her first novel, *Wise Blood* (1952), that established her as a unique and powerful talent with a genius for the humorous and the grotesque. Miss O'Connor is also the author of *A Good Man Is Hard to Find* (stories) and *The Violent Bear It Away.* She died in 1964 at the age of thirty-eight. *Flannery O'Connor: The Complete Stories,* a collection of thirty-one stories, received the National Book Award for fiction in 1972.

TILLIE OLSEN was born in Nebraska in 1913 and has lived in San Francisco since 1933. Her life and identification are primarily working class. She wrote as a girl, was a Depression high school dropout, but having to work as well as raise four children, was not able to resume writing until she was in her forties. She is the author of *Tell Me a Riddle,* a short story collection whose title piece won the O. Henry Award as Best Short Story of the Year in 1961, and *Requa,* a portion of which appeared in *Best American Short Stories, 1971.* She has received a Ford Foundation and a National Endowment for the Arts grant, and was a member of the Radcliffe Institute in 1962–64.

KATHERINE ANNE PORTER was born in Texas in 1894 and grew up there and in New Orleans. She has taught and lectured in many colleges and universities, both in the United States and in Europe. Miss Porter has long been recognized as one of America's most distinguished authors. Her works include *Flowering Judas and Other Stories, Pale Horse, Pale Rider, The Leaning Tower and Other Stories,* and *Ship of Fools.* She won both a Pulitzer Prize and a National Book Award in 1966 for her *Collected Stories* and was awarded the Gold Medal for Fiction by the National Institute of Arts and Letters in 1967.

DATE DUE

DEC 4 '81 S			
DEC 2 8 PM			
MAR 15 '82 S			
AUG 25 '83 S			
JUN 14 '95 S			
JUN 12 1996			
JUN 1 97 S			
JUL 0 7 1997			
GAYLORD			PRINTED IN U.S A.